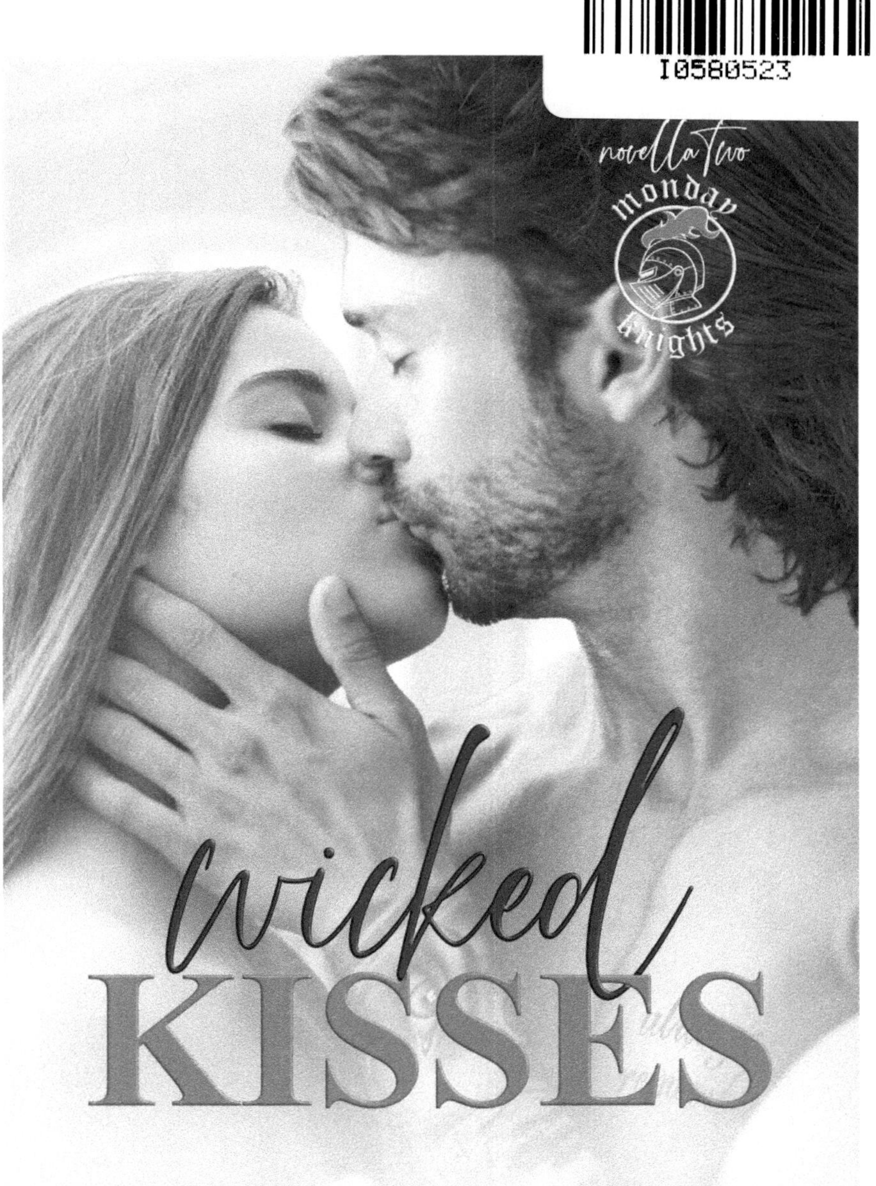

novella two
monday knights
wicked
KISSES
DEBRA ST JAMES

Wicked Kisses

MONDAY KNIGHTS — NOVELLA TWO

DEBRA ST JAMES

Website: www.debrastjamesbooks.com

Email: debrastjamesbooks@gmail.com

Published by: Debra St James Author

Formatted by: Debra St James Author

ISBN: 978-1-923153-09-7 [Paperback]

ISBN: 978-1-923153-10-3 [Discreet Edition Paperback]

ISBN: 978-1-923153-08-0 [Ebook]

inspiration

This story was inspired by the lyrics …

—> *Blow by Ed Sheeran with Chris Stapleton & Bruno Mars* <—

playlist

BLOW … *Ed Sheeran, Chris Stapleton, Bruno Mars*
Owner of a Lonely Heart … *Yes*
Bedroom Eyes … *Kate Ceberano*
Every Little Thing She Does … *The Police*
She Drives Me Crazy … *Fine Young Cannibals*
You Shook Me All Night Long … *AC/DC*
Need You Tonight … *INXS*
Good Thing … *Fine Young Cannibals*
You Give Me Something … *Jamiroquai*
Devil in a Dress … *Teddy Swims*
Beautiful Girl … *INXS*

You can check it out here:
https://tinyurl.com/wickedkisses-spotify

CHAPTER 1

—sophie—

I BOUNCE INTO THE KITCHEN, KISS DAD ON HIS BRISTLY CHEEK, and grab a green apple from the fruit bowl. Without looking up from his newspaper, he smiles as I take a noisy bite of the crunchy fruit. "What are you up to today, Soph?"

"I have a job interview." Butterflies erupt in my stomach when I say the words. This could be the beginning of my dream come true.

His eyebrows rise and he drops the paper to the table. "Whereabouts?"

I swallow and fake nonchalance—"*Fine Line Art Studio.*"— then take another bite of my apple as I wait for him to forbid me from going; it wouldn't be the first time.

He rolls back from the table with a proud smile and then pushes himself toward me. "Well, I wish you luck. It'll be fantastic to see you put your art degree to good use."

I blow out a relieved breath and carry James's breakfast dishes to the sink. *I don't know how many times I've asked that kid to clean up after himself.* "Thanks, Dad. I'm a little nervous." Obviously, he doesn't realize what type of art studio it is—a small blessing.

Creases form between his bushy brows as they dip. "Why on earth are you nervous? You graduated top of your fine arts class. Any art studio would be lucky to have you. You've been wasting your talent working as a receptionist at *Beyond the Fringe*." *I know, but at least Marina gave me a job even though I had no clue about working in a hairdressing salon.*

My heart floats with his praise. "Thanks, Dad. You're the best." I lean down and wrap my arms around his shoulders. "Anyway, I'd better get going." I grab my portfolio and toss my backpack over my shoulder.

"Good luck!" he calls as I close the front door behind me.

With giddiness erupting in my stomach, I skip down the ramp, throw my stuff onto the passenger seat, and climb behind the wheel of my car. Taking deep breaths to calm my racing heart, I put my car in drive and head for the city, blasting my favorite playlist to distract myself from my impending interview at one of the best tattoo studios in the city. I want this job with a desperation I haven't felt in a long time. Art is my passion and pieces of my soul have slowly crumbled away with every phone I answer and hair appointment I book at the salon.

I pull into the parking lot down the road from *Fine Line* and grab my stuff, then lock my car. Walking into the mall, I head straight for the bathroom and step into an empty stall. Dragging my ripped jeans out of my backpack, I slide my feet out of my ballet flats, and replace my A-line skirt, then strip out of my button-up sweater and cotton blouse and push my arms into my black silk shirt, tying it to show a sliver of my stomach. I shove my feet into my purple Converse high tops, then mess around with my dark hair, adding volume and making the waves look messy and unkempt. Once I'm happy with that, I add eyeliner around my eyes and a red stain to my lips. I carefully pack everything into my backpack, ensuring it won't crease so I can change before I go home.

When I look at myself in the mirror, I almost don't recognize the woman staring back at me. It's been a long time since I dressed like this. Almost nine years, if I'm counting. Nine years ago, I tucked my true self away after getting pregnant by my high school boyfriend and disappointing my father. I became the straight-laced, well-behaved daughter he deserved and have worked my ass off to be the best mom I can be. I never wanted to see that look on my father's face again, and I promised myself I would always toe the line and make better choices.

Applying for this job has renewed my worry that I'll disappoint my father, but I'm struggling to suppress the real me; my soul is dying little by little and I'm convinced there'll be nothing left by the time I turn thirty. My church-going father frowns upon people who have tattoos, judging them harshly based on the art adorning their bodies. I, on the other hand, adore tattoos. I love how individual they are and the stories they tell. How the gorgeous designs shift and change as the muscle moves beneath the flesh.

I suck in a long breath and blow it out slowly, then head back to my car to dump my backpack and grab my portfolio.

Here goes nothing.

I walk down the dirty sidewalk with confident steps—*fake it 'til you make it, right?*—and pass a guy who's probably more than a foot taller than me, leaning against the red brick wall while he talks on his phone. Large windows next to him offer me a view inside the studio and I pause to look. My lips tip up with approval as my heart hammers a nervous rhythm. I've seen some dingy tattoo places, but this one is classy; all clean lines, modern design, and soft edges created by greenery.

The deep timbre of the guy's voice causes a shiver to run down my spine and has me glancing toward him. His dark, messy hair has fallen forward, shielding him from my view, but I can see enough to know he has just the right amount of facial scruff—my kryptonite. He's dressed in black, from his combat boots to the black T-shirt stretched across his broad chest, leaving his tattooed arms exposed. Stepping around him, I rub my sweaty palm on my jeans, then open the door to the studio and walk inside, breathing deeply and working to maintain an air of confidence. I stop at the counter and readjust my portfolio tucked beneath my arm.

"Linc will be with you in a sec." I spin toward the voice and come face to face with a bald man sporting a beard that could rival Santa's. "Take a seat, doll." He winks at me, then drops his head to focus on the ass he's tattooing. One cheek is rather hairy, so I'm assuming he had to shave the one he's working on. I shudder a little on the inside. But I'll have to take the good with the bad, right? I'll finally be using my art daily and people will be inked forever with my designs. I can put up with a dude's hairy ass now and then.

The guy from outside storms in through the door, letting it bang loudly behind him. Anger and frustration radiate from him as he passes, making the air around me vibrate. His mood matches the color of his clothes, and I wonder if it was the phone call that upset him or if he's always an angry storm.

"Hey, Linc. Can you help our visitor?" The older tattoo artist calls out. Linc glares at me over his shoulder with a furrowed brow and I sit up straighter, holding my portfolio tightly in my lap as if it can protect me somehow.

Linc—*Lincoln*.

He's the boss.

He's the one I've been dealing with via email.

The one I'm here to see.

I swallow past the lump in my throat and try to fight my nerves. He seemed so … easygoing over email, but there's nothing easygoing about him in person. He's downright intimidating. Damn it. I don't know if I can do this.

C'mon Soph.

This is your dream job. You can do this. He's probably a

soft teddy bear beneath all that angry energy, black fabric, and heavy boots.

Lincoln steps through a doorway and disappears from my sight and I collapse against the back of the green velvet-covered couch, blowing out a harsh breath. I don't understand how his mood seemed to follow him through the place like a wave cresting and crashing on the shore. There was a violence about him that was impossible to miss and I frown at my lap as I consider the possibility of working alongside someone with so much negative energy.

"Don't worry, doll. He's mostly all bark," the older guy calls across to me with a chuckle.

I try to smile and laugh at his obvious attempt at a joke, but I doubt I pull it off.

—lincoln—

"I'M ASKING YOU TO STOP, LINC. PLEASE," MOM BEGS AS I rest my foot against the wall outside my studio.

"I can't. It's been part of me for so long. I don't know who I am without it." Out of the corner of my eye, I notice a pint-sized woman peering in through my studio windows. She may be short, but she has curves in all the right places—*damn*. And that long, thick hair. I'm a sucker for beautiful hair. An image of wrapping my fist through the strands and pushing her to her knees assaults me out of nowhere.

"It's been thirty-one years tomorrow. I miss her too. Don't you think pieces of my heart aren't missing? She was *my* baby girl." Her sigh rings out across the line and the pocket-sized woman steps inside my studio. "Every time you fight, you dredge up all the pain again … I worry I'll lose you too. I can't keep doing this, Linc. Can't you see that you're causing more harm than good?"

Like I need to be reminded what tomorrow is. It's not like I'll ever forget. I exhale a long breath. I hear what she's saying, but I can't stop. I don't want to. It's my way of coping. "I gotta go, Mom."

"Okay, Linc. Remember, I love you."

"Love you too, Mom." I disconnect the call and push off the wall, running my hand through my hair to push it out of my face. I need a fucking haircut, but the chick I normally see has moved south to be with her boyfriend, and I'm fussy about who cuts it.

Dragging open the heavy wood and glass door to the studio, I storm through and let it bang behind me. I can't believe she wants me to give up my fights. I'm only gonna stop when my body can't do it anymore, but maybe I shouldn't tell her about them. Let her think I've given it up. I doubt I'll be fighting too much longer, anyway.

"Hey, Linc. Can you help our visitor?" Ken calls from his station, pointing toward our waiting area. I peer over my shoulder at the pint-sized chick I saw enter—now that I look at her properly, she seems young, really young. She's sitting straight as a board, clutching a folder tightly on her lap. I keep walking and step into the office to give myself a moment to collect myself. I'm sure the college chick can wait a few minutes before I have to discuss yet another butterfly tattoo. What is it with girls and butterfly tattoos? Why can't they be a little more creative?

My phone vibrates in my pocket and I drag it out to read the screen. "Shit." I completely forgot about the interview with Sophie.

The back door to the studio opens and Jenna steps inside. "Hey, Linc."

"Hey. How are you feeling?" I narrow my eyes and study her closely.

"Tired. And look at my feet." She shoves her foot at me, but I don't know what I'm supposed to be looking at. She shakes it around, lifts her other foot, and repeats the process. "I don't have ankles anymore," she complains.

Oh, yeah. I guess she doesn't. "Damn." I laugh and she whacks me playfully across the chest.

Her eyes go all dreamy as she rubs her very round stomach. "If I didn't love this bean so much, I'd be pissed at how much my body has changed."

"Pretty sure it's bigger than a bean now," I raise my eyebrows and pointedly look at the size of her belly. I'm not sure how she's standing upright. "What are you doing here, anyway? You're supposed to be home resting."

She waves off my comment. "I'm bored. There's nothing to do."

"I think that's the point, Jen." She shrugs. "You wanna do a consult while you're here? I'm waiting on the woman I'm supposed to interview for your position, and there's a college chick out front."

Her lips tip up and her eyes sparkle. "Sure." She waddles to the front of the studio and I pull out a sheet of paper to design a mechanical sleeve tattoo for a new client. I glance at the time. Sophie's late. That's strike one. I dislike tardiness.

I press the tip of my pencil to the paper, ready to make the first stroke. "The chick out front says she's here for the interview," Jenna says as she leans against the door. "Says her name's Sophie."

I spin in my chair to look at her. "Can't be. She told me she's twenty-six. That chick can't be over twenty."

"Why would she say she's here for an interview if she isn't?" Her lips tip up in that mischievous way of hers. "She's gorgeous."

Damn. At least she wasn't late, but I doubt she'll fit in here. I didn't notice any ink—a tattoo artist *should* have ink. It's bad for business if they don't. I blow out a harsh breath and rise to my feet. "You wanna sit in on the interview?"

"Nah. I'm gonna window shop for a bit, then go home and take a nap before Dean gets home."

"All right. Let me know if there's anything you need." She leaves out the back door and I step out of the office to meet with Sophie. This should be interesting. My first instinct is to tell her to fuck off for wasting my time. The only problem is that I'm short-staffed, and the samples of her artwork were spectacular. When I step through the door to the front of the studio, she has her head down, looking at something on her phone, the folder she was clutching when I walked in, balanced precariously on her lap. "Sophie?"

Her head snaps up, and she rises to her feet, clumsily gripping the folder. "Yes. Uh … hi. Yeah, I'm uh Sophie."

I suppress my grin at her awkwardness and hold out my hand. "Hi, I'm Lincoln. Would you like to come through to my office? We can get started."

"Sure. Yeah, uh that'd be great." I lead her through to my office, and her eyes widen as she scans the photographs on the walls, displaying some of our best work. "These are incredible." She steps closer to the life-size photograph of my back and presses her hand to her chest. "This one is full of pain, with that dark angel standing protectively over the little girl." Her eyes trace the image. "Those wings look like they could open, and he could fly away at any moment. The detail is incredible." She says the last part softly, more to herself than to me.

I move next to her. "That's some of Ken's work. The old guy out front." She turns her head to look at me, and I realize how close I'm standing. I thought her eyes were a simple color, but a ring of darker brown surrounds the lighter brown center with striations almost the color of coffee. Her lips part, and my gaze drops to the red-stained pillows. *I wonder what color they are without all the crap on them?* Shoving my hands in my front pockets, I step back and raise my chin to the chair opposite my desk. "Please take a seat, and we'll get started."

She makes herself comfortable and slides the folder she's

holding across the table. "I thought I'd bring my full portfolio for you to see."

I leave it sitting in the middle of my desk. "I thought you said you were twenty-six on your application."

She straightens her spine, adding another inch to her height. "I am."

"You look younger."

"I can show you a copy of my birth certificate if you don't believe me," she fires back. She's no pushover. I like that. "I didn't think to bring it with me. What does my age matter, anyway?"

I shrug. "Just don't want someone who's not gonna be reliable, and I find kids can be flaky."

"Well, I'm not a kid, and I'm not flaky," she says firmly. "You can always rely on me to be on time, to do what's expected, if not more, and to take responsibility for any mistakes and work toward not making them again." She shrugs, raising a single brow. "I'm the best person for this position, Mr. Kingsley. You won't be sorry." *Mr. Kingsley.*

I appreciate her candor, and I know Ken will, too. I reach forward to collect her folder, sliding it closer. Without taking my eyes off the girl opposite me, I flip open the cover. I've already seen the pieces she attached to her application, but neither of those prepared me for the first illustration. Her talent and line work are exceptional. She'll be a fantastic asset to our team, providing an alternate style of artwork from Ken and me. "How long have you been drawing?"

"Since I was a kid. Then I studied art in high school and finally specialized in fine arts at community college." Her eyes scan the tattoo on my arm, and she lifts her chin toward it. "Who did that?"

I point toward the front room. "Ken."

Her eyebrows rise. "He's good."

"That he is." I study her closely. "You don't seem to have any art."

Defensiveness shadows her features. "Not that you can see."

That piques my interest. "So you *do* have art?"

Tucking her thick hair behind her ear, her eyes dart from one side to the other. "Yeah. Why?"

"It wouldn't sit well with me if you didn't have any art. It would suggest to me *and* our clients that you're not a fan of tattoos." I lift and drop one shoulder, tilting my head to the side. "It would come across as hypocritical." I wait for her to argue—she doesn't seem the type to take a comment like that lying down.

"Well, I have art," she snaps.

I raise my brows, waiting for her to expand, but she isn't forthcoming. "Right. How much tattoo experience have you had?"

She readjusts her position and studies the artwork behind my desk with great interest. "None," she murmurs.

Surely I didn't hear that correctly. I flip open her application and drag my eyes down the page. "It says here that you worked at *artWORX* for two years."

"Yeah, that's correct." She swallows, and I watch her slender throat move.

"As a …" I raise my eyebrows and leave the sentence hanging for her to finish.

Turning her head to the side, she finally responds. "Receptionist."

Damn it! I knew she was too good to be true. "This position is for a receptionist-slash-tattoo artist."

"I know." Pushing her shoulders back and sitting taller, she looks me in the eye. "I'm a fast learner, Mr. Kingsley." Shit, if she keeps calling me that, I won't be able to keep my hard-on at bay. "I already have the artistic ability. I just need to learn how to use the gun."

I run my hands through my messy hair. This isn't going how I thought it would. I stand abruptly, pushing my chair back so it bangs against the wall. "This isn't a trainee opportunity." I rest the tips of my fingers on my desk and lean forward—I'm sure from her lowered position I'm intimidating, but she doesn't budge. "It's not as simple as learning how to use the gun. There's technique, shading, color, design, communication, infection control, knowledge of the skin and muscles, wound care, scarring … there's so fucking much to know. It's not just drawing on flesh." This sort of attitude frustrates the shit out of me.

She stands too. "I *know* that. I *want* to learn. I've already been studying how to identify common skin diseases and how scarred skin can take ink. I *know* I need to have exceptional communication skills during every step of the process. I've been teaching myself the best hygiene practices, and I learned a fair amount during my time at *artWORX*. You can count on me. I need this job. I *want* this job. I was born to do this type of work."

Her words bleed with genuine passion and desire, and while common sense tells me this isn't what I need for the studio, I can't deny her artistic talent, her self-belief, or her desire for this opportunity. I blow out a long, frustrated breath and look away, giving myself time to think—something I can't do while she's looking at me with those bedroom eyes of hers. Standing upright, I push my hair back with agitation, and when I turn my gaze back toward her, I catch her watching me closely. "I'll need to discuss this with Ken. I'll call you one way or the other tonight."

Her shoulders sag, and the scent of defeat fills the air, replacing her coconut scent as she leans across my desk, using the tips of her fingers to drag her portfolio back toward her.

"You know, it's hard to get experience when nobody's prepared to give you a chance to get it." She closes the folder. "Thank you for your time, Mr. Kingsley."

And with that parting sentence, she reminds me what an asshole I am. She hoists her purse over her shoulder and leaves my office without another word. My eyes drop to her perfect ass. It's probably for the best if I don't give her the position. She's far too enticing. The way she stood up to me was hot as fuck. Add in her artistic talent and the package she comes in, and she's way too tempting for a guy like me.

CHAPTER 3

—sophie—

"Mom, why can't I have a phone? All my friends have them. I'm the only kid at school that doesn't have one." I roll my eyes at his dramatics, knowing he's not the only kid without a phone. "If I had a phone, I'd be able to let you know where I am when we're not together."

"I already know where you are when we're not together. You're at school or you're here with Grandad." I ruffle his hair with a chuckle. "You don't need a phone, James. Not yet. Stop being in such a rush to grow up. I'm not ready."

"But, Mom." He slaps his hands against his thighs.

I drag my fingers through my hair. "No. I'm not discussing this with you again until you're at least twelve."

"Damn." He pouts.

"Mouth."

He huffs and I smile internally. I know I'm doing my job properly when he gets pissed at me. James, my pride and joy, stomps his way down the hallway. "Don't forget to bring your homework back with you," I call after him.

Dad rolls out of his office, shaking his head. "You're doing a great job with him."

"Thanks, Dad. I'm doing my best; even if *he* doesn't think so."

I head into the kitchen to prepare our afternoon snacks, so James and I can work on his homework. I'm unsure what my schedule will be if I get this job—which I doubt—so I make the most of my free afternoon. The kid who steps into the kitchen has done a three-sixty from the one who stomped away from me. "Sorry, Mom. I'll stop asking for a phone."

"I'd appreciate it." Another phone plan isn't in the budget.

We sit at the table and tackle his homework as he snacks. While he works on his math grids, my mind wanders to my interview with Lincoln Kingsley. The man oozes authority and masculinity. I couldn't keep my eyes from tracing every inch of him, especially the beautifully designed piece on his left arm. What I wouldn't give to ink some of my designs onto someone's flesh, but I guess it's never going to happen since I need to have experience to get a job as a tattoo artist. Lord only knows how I'm supposed to do that.

"Mom, do you think this is right?" James breaks into my thoughts.

I study the grid closely. "All the squares seem to complete the equations correctly."

His lips spread. "Yay!" He thrusts his fist upward in celebration.

I chuckle. "All right. You'd better write the answers in the spaces."

We keep working, testing his spelling words and I listen to him read his latest reader. "Okay. I think that's everything. Pack all of this away and you can have one hour on your Xbox."

He quickly stands, packs his backpack ready for school tomorrow, and races into the front room to turn on his game. As I wash my hands, Dad rolls into the kitchen. "How did your interview go this morning?"

"The owner said he'd call, but I'm not holding my breath. He wants someone with experience, and that isn't me."

Dad's eyebrows draw low over his eyes as they narrow in thought. "But you've been drawing a long time. What more do they need?"

I rub at an already clean spot on the counter and shrug. "I guess they need hands-on experience. Something I don't have."

He rolls closer and tips my chin up so I can't avoid his eyes. "Well, if they can't see the talented young lady you are, then that's their loss. Other positions will become available and perhaps the next boss will appreciate you for the talent that you are."

My heart expands to almost double its size and warmth fills me. "Thanks, Dad." If only he knew where I was trying to get a job, he'd probably be happy with my lack of success.

I prepare enchiladas for dinner and we eat as James tells us about his day, then Dad shares the idea for a twist that came to him today for his latest work in progress. It's great to see him excited about this book. He had a hard time in the beginning as he was trying to work out his character's motivation and the events that would need to take place before the conspiracy is revealed. But it seems he's on track now. After we finish eating, I wash the dishes, while James dries, and Dad makes chocolate pudding cups for dessert.

James and I get comfortable on the couch and Dad plays the next episode of *Dirty Jobs*, James's favorite TV show. We're about halfway through the episode when my phone startles me. I snatch it from the side table and my heart skips. It's Lincoln. I honestly didn't expect him to call. "I need to take this. Back in a moment." I kiss the top of James's head and hurry from the room. Pressing the button with a shaky finger, I take the call. "Hello, this is Sophie." I roll my eyes. *He already knows who you are; he phoned you.*

His warm chuckle sounds across the phone and my cheeks heat. I don't know what it is about him, but I seem to become a blathering idiot in his presence. "Hi, Sophie. Is this a good time to chat?"

"Depends whether you're calling with good or bad news." I slap my forehead. *Shut up, Soph.* "Sorry. Yeah, I can talk now."

"Great. I spoke with Ken after you left and he's happy to help me train you. We'll have to balance it with your reception work and it'll require you to spend some of your time at the studio in the role of a student, which isn't a paid position. When you come in to complete your paperwork, we'll work out a schedule that'll work for you and the studio."

Surely I heard him wrong. "Di-did you just offer me the job?"

He chuckles again, and the sound vibrates through every cell of my body. "Yeah. I just offered you the job."

"Ohmygodohmygodohmygod. Thank you so much!" My cheeks stretch as far as they can go. "You have no idea how much this means to me." I jump up and down on the spot. "Thank you so much. I promise I won't let you down. I'll be the best trainee you've ever had."

"You're welcome. Ken and I couldn't ignore your artistic talent. Your style is unique, and you made it clear how much you want the position. When can you come in to sign your paperwork and work out a schedule?"

"Oh, um, I have to work tomorrow. I could come by after six if you're available."

"Hang on, I'll check my schedule." Silence fills the phone as I pace the hallway with excited steps. "Yeah, that should work."

I blow out a breath. "Great. Thank you so much. I promise you won't be sorry."

"I hope not. See you tomorrow." He disconnects the call

before I can respond, and I'm left staring at my phone as the screen fades to black. *Did he sound pissed off?* I don't even care. I got the freaking job of my dreams!

I spin around, throw my arms up, and shimmy my ass. I can't believe it. I could have sworn I had no hope of getting the job when I left the interview. I won't be able to sleep tonight. Stepping into the living room, I try to contain my excitement so I don't interrupt the show, but I can't stop my leg from shaking up and down.

In the ad break, Dad asks, "What was that about?"

My cheeks rise. "I got the job."

James immediately jumps up on the couch and bounces. "Congratulations, Mom. That's awesome."

"Thank you. I think it's pretty awesome too, but that's no reason to jump on the couch." I give him my best mom eyes and he drops to his butt with a sheepish grin. This kid owns my heart, but he'll find any excuse to push the boundaries.

"Congratulations. When do you start?" Dad asks.

"I need to stop by after work tomorrow to complete the paperwork and I guess we'll work out a start date. I'll give my notice at work in the morning."

"I'm proud of you, Mom."

I wrap my arm around my son and pull him in close, kissing the top of his head. "Thanks, James. That means a lot to me."

"We'll have to stop by and visit you. Introduce ourselves to your boss." Dad rolls closer to me and lays his hand on my knee. "I'm proud of you, Soph. You work toward your goals and you're making things happen the way you want." He pushes back. "This calls for a celebration. Hot chocolate all around."

"Ah, Dad, thanks, but I don't think it'd be a good idea," I call to his back. "I need to settle in and get used to everything first. I don't know what the policy is for visitors at work."

He waves me off. "We'll give you time to settle in. Don't worry."

Oh shit!

CHAPTER 4

—lincoln—

I drop my keys on the entry table and close the front door behind me, then head straight to the kitchen to grab a beer and go in search of Aaron. I don't have to look far; finding him in the living room with his leg propped up on the coffee table, ice wrapped around his knee.

"What the fuck happened to you?" I snap.

"Turned awkwardly at work and twisted my knee. Pretty sure I heard a *pop*."

I grimace. "Shit, that doesn't sound good."

"Nope. Hurts like a bitch."

I hold up my beer. "You want me to get you one?"

"Nah. Thanks. I took some painkillers, so I probably shouldn't drink."

I nod, then drop to the opposite end of the couch. "Are they gonna be able to manage without you for a while?"

"Yeah. I have the place running like a well-oiled machine. I can take a couple of days off." I take a drink and drop my head against the back of the couch, blowing out a long breath. "You had the interviews today, right?" I nod without lifting my head. "How'd they go?"

"Yeah, good … I guess. I offered the female candidate the job."

He looks at me closely. "You don't sound convinced."

"Because I'm not." I exhale a long breath.

He sits forward, wincing. "Then why'd you give her the job?"

"Her artistic talent is phenomenal." I take another drink.

Aaron adjusts the ice pack. "What's the problem, then?"

"She's never held a tattoo gun."

"Shit!"

"Yeah." I fidget with the label on the bottle. "I needed someone to walk in and start tattooing from day one, which isn't gonna happen with this chick."

"What about the other applicant?"

I shake my head. "I don't know what it was about her that made me offer her the job." I look at my long-time friend. "Her design skills are top-notch. Her eye for detail and color … man … fucking remarkable. But there was another guy who was pretty good and could have walked straight into the job. He just didn't seem to have that … *passion* that Sophie had."

"I hear ya. Sometimes passion for the job outweighs the other stuff. Do you think she'll pick it up quickly?"

"I do. Ken and I spoke about it after she left and after some convincing, he's happy to train her. I told her we wouldn't pay her for the training and she was happy to accept."

He raises a brow. "That says a lot."

"It says everything." I finish my beer. "Anyway, I'm heading out for a fight. You need anything before I go?"

"Nah, I'm good. I'll probably go to bed soon. Hopefully, I can sleep off the pain." He readjusts the ice pack again. "Be careful, hey."

I stand. "I'm always careful."

He barks out a laugh. "Bullshit."

I toss my empty bottle in the trash and head for the door. "Night."

"Night."

I climb to my feet and rub my jaw; sweat rolls in rivulets down my torso. I flick my damp hair out of my eyes and raise my hands, protecting my face. He lunges and I dance out of the way, then duck to jab him in the ribs, knocking him off balance. Before he can regain his footing, I kick out at his obliques, then follow up with a round kick to his head as he staggers, and he drops to the mat like a stone.

Blood trickles from his nose as the referee squats next to him and rubs his hand across his lifeless back. He swipes his arms across his body and euphoria sweeps through me.

I don't come here to lose.

I don't put my body through the rigors of kickboxing to be the loser.

My opponent talked a big game tonight, but he didn't have the stamina to support his smack talk, something I never do. It's a waste of energy. I'd rather let my body do the talking in the ring.

His coach climbs into the ring to tend to him while the referee holds up my arm and announces me as the winner to a roaring crowd. When I climb out, Ken hands over my water bottle and pats me on the back. "You looked great up there, Linc."

"Thanks. Felt good. I thought this guy was supposed to be a challenge." I smirk.

He shrugs, looking at the guy laid flat out. "What can I say? You're on fire." He chuckles as we make our way to the locker room. Once I'm changed into my street clothes, we head out. "You wanna grab a drink?"

I adjust the bag on my shoulder. "Nah, I need to go home and work on the books for the studio."

He shakes his head. "Man, I don't miss those days."

The organizer, Mike, approaches us. "Congrats, Linc. You want the money deposited into the usual account?"

"Thanks. Yeah, always the same account."

He nods and chews his thumbnail. "I was calculating. You've won almost a million since you started fighting ten years ago."

My eyes almost bulge out of my sockets. I hadn't been keeping track. "That's impressive."

"You could have bought yourself a fancy home close to the bay for that," Ken says as he slaps my back.

I shake my head. "Nah. This is more important than buying a fancy house." Ken knows how important this money is to me and how much it helps the people who need it more than I do. It's the only reason I fight, even if I started fighting as a release when I was an angry teen.

It's been a shit day.

April seventh is always a shit day, but my mood has been darker than usual. Ken normally ignores my moods, but even *he* had enough and called me out on my shit; something he hasn't done since I first started working for him. I kicked my ass, reeled in my emotions, and concentrated on my art after apologizing profusely to my mentor and long-time friend.

Six o'clock sharp, the bell over the door rings and when I glance up, Sophie's standing in the doorway, looking as stunning as I remember. When she sees me, her face lights with a smile, weirdly smoothing out a jagged piece of my heart. I groan under my breath because that smile is going to be hazardous for my sanity. I climb to my feet to greet her as Ken waltzes past me, straight for her with a wide grin and open arms. I swear, the guy is an enormous teddy bear.

"Hey, doll. Congrats on the job. I saw your work and can't wait to see it permanently marked on someone's skin. I may even let you ink me." He winks and wraps his tattoo-covered arms around her, taking her by surprise.

Surprise gone, she smiles and raises her arms to return his embrace. "Thank you. I'm so excited to work with you guys." She points behind him toward my office. "I saw your work on the wall in Lincoln's office. You're crazy talented."

The old guy blushes at her compliment. Something I've never seen him do. I step closer to them and her attention finally falls back on me. Her eyes widen and she steps forward, raising her hand to my chin as her brows dip low over those gorgeous eyes of hers that are now filled with concern. "What happened to you?"

Her fingers make gentle contact and I suck in a breath at the electricity that sparks from that simple touch. She tilts my chin toward the light and I'm sure it looks bad. The guy got in a decent hit before I laid him flat. I shrug. "I was in a fight last night."

She snatches her hand away like she's been struck by lightning and her eyes narrow with suspicion. "Oh."

When people discover I fight, they make assumptions about me and I rarely care to correct them. It's not my business what people think of me. But for some reason, I don't want her to think I spend my time brawling in pubs and bars. "It was a planned fight … in a ring … with a referee." I rush to add.

One side of Ken's mouth tips up as he raises a single bushy brow.

Her shoulders drop and the suspicion that colored her

features a moment ago slides away. "What sort of fighting do you do?"

"Kickboxing. Usually, once a month. Maybe twice, if I'm lucky to have my name drawn out of the pool."

She huffs. "Lucky?"

"Yeah, lucky." I fold my arms across my chest and her eyes drop to my forearms. She scans the artwork with appreciation and I flex my muscle because the tiger's eye looks fucking awesome when I do that.

Sophie gasps and glances up at Ken. "You did this?" He nods with pride. "It's incredible."

"You should see Linc's back. Some of my best work." She looks at me as if she wants me to turn around and expose my back. *Maybe if she shows me hers, I'll show her mine.*

I snap out of my salacious thoughts. "We'd better sign the paperwork so you can head home. I have a client coming at seven."

She tucks her long, brown hair behind her ear and that vision of my hand tangled in it hits me right between the eyes. "Yeah, sure. I don't want to hold you up."

I hold out my hand toward my office and she leads the way. My eyes drop to the curve of that sweet ass of hers and I bite my bottom lip.

She's too fucking young for you. Stop looking at her ass.

She takes her seat opposite my desk and I pull out the folder I prepared earlier today with everything I need. I explain everything and she completes her details—even showing me her birth certificate—and signs her name on the dotted line with an artistic flourish.

"We're closed Sunday and Monday. Open 'til seven Tuesday and Wednesday and 'til ten Thursday through Saturday nights, unless I have a fight or a late booking. We open at ten every day." She nods, biting her bottom lip. "I don't have a receptionist after six. We turn on the answering machine and catch up on any calls in the morning. So, I'll need you here Tuesday through to Saturday, nine forty-five 'til six." She nods again, but she's a little more relaxed. Maybe she didn't like the idea of the late evenings. "Some nights you may need to stay later, but we'll sort that out as we go. Any questions?"

She looks conflicted, but shakes her head. "When can I start?"

"As soon as possible. How much notice do you need to give your current employer?"

"I gave my notice this morning. Marina's thrilled that I've landed the job of my dreams and said they'd manage if I needed to start right away."

For the first time today, a grin touches my lips and my shoulders drop an inch or two. "Great. How about Tuesday?"

Her smile is genuine except for the red paint on her lips. "Tuesday's perfect. Thank you so much for this opportunity. I promise you won't regret it." She stands and holds her hand out across my desk, so I stand, too.

"I hope not." I engulf her small hand with my much larger one and that same spark of energy bursts up my arm and spreads across my chest.

Creases form between her brows. "You keep saying that. Why did you offer me the job if you're not convinced?" She pulls her hand away and I want to reach across and take it again.

I consider my answer and watch her squirm a little as she waits. "I need someone who could take a station and tattoo from day one. I have bookings backed up for months. But I couldn't ignore your talent and enthusiasm for the job. We need to get you up to speed fast. Do you think you're up for the challenge?"

She nods enthusiastically and tucks her hands in the back

pockets of her jeans, pushing her tits out. "Absolutely. I *know* I can do this."

I nod. "See you Tuesday. Don't be late." She frowns, but turns on her heel. "Oh, and Sophie." I wait until she turns back to face me. "Welcome to the team."

Creases form at the corners of her eyes. "Thank you. You'll never know how much this opportunity means to me."

She drops her head and leaves my office and I fall into my chair, pushing my hair out of my face. This job seems to mean a lot to her and if I can work with her to reach her potential, she'll be a kick-ass tattoo artist.

CHAPTER 5

—*sophie*—

Nine thirty-five stares up at me when I glance at my phone. I was determined to get here early since Lincoln thinks I'll struggle to be on time. I have a point to prove and I'm going to do everything I can to show him he didn't make a mistake when he hired me.

Telling Dad I started at nine-fifteen to allow myself enough time to change on the way here was tough. I hate lying to him, but what's another lie on top of the biggest of them all? I'm not sure what's going to happen when he finds out what my new job is—because he'll eventually find out. I only hope by then, I'll be a tattoo artist with a reputation for doing incredible work and he'll be proud of me.

I push the door but it's locked, so I knock on the glass and peer into the dark interior. When nobody answers after a few moments, I knock louder because maybe they're in the back office. I noticed a fancy coffee machine in the tiny kitchen area on Friday, so I'd guess they start their day there. Disappointment grows when there's still no answer. Stepping back from the building, I peer down the street and wonder if there's an entrance around the back. Heading toward the alley between two buildings, I make my way down it, ignoring the trash and wrinkling my nose at the powerful stench of urine. God, people are gross. The alley opens up to a parking lot, and it's easy to find the door to *Fine Line* since it matches the rest of the place. There's a burnt orange Chevelle parked in one of the bays, so I knock on the back door. Heavy footfalls sound on the polished concrete inside, and I blow out a breath to settle my nerves. When the door opens, my hot new boss is standing there. His bright blue eyes latch onto me and his eyebrows shoot up.

I focus solely on his face to stop my gaze from wandering down his fit body, which would be completely inappropriate. "Morning." I smile past my nervousness.

"Morning," he mumbles as he steps aside to allow me in.

"I knocked at the front door but there was no answer, so I thought I'd try my luck here," I explain as I step past him. His soft cedar scent wafts around me, calming me slightly. "Is there somewhere I can leave my purse, and where would you like me to start?" I ask.

He chuckles and the raspiness of it makes a direct hit in my lower belly. Crinkles form at the corner of his eyes and creases bracket his mouth beneath his stubble, which has a few white hairs here and there. "Slow down, Shortcake." *Shortcake?* I narrow my eyes at him and he waves his hand down the length of my body with raised brows. "You're short." *Ugh!* I know he's head and shoulders taller than me, but I'm not *that* short. I mean, maybe I am. I'm only five foot … five-five if I'm wearing my favorite boots. He waves his arm out toward the coffee machine. "Make yourself a cup and we'll go through the expectations for today."

The machine is straightforward, so I make myself a coffee in a spare cup I find at the back of the cupboard—note to self, bring a cup from home—and plonk down in the chair opposite

Linc's desk. Taking my first sip, I close my eyes in appreciation. When I open them again, Lincoln is watching me with a hint of amusement.

"That first sip is always the best." I nod and watch him take a sip of his coffee, admiring the movement of his Adam's apple beneath his dark stubble. He studies me closely, and I barely resist squirming under his intense oceanic gaze. "How are you feeling about today?"

My shoulders drop and my cheeks lift. "Nervous-excited but ready to get started and learn all the things."

"Good." He leans forward in his chair. "Jenna's coming in for an hour or so to show you the computer booking system and how we take payments. Then Ken is going to show you how to set up a station because you'll be responsible for keeping our stations prepped."

"That's similar to what I had to do at *artWORX* and the salon, so it'll be easy to pick up." I'm confident I can learn this job quickly.

"Good. In between answering phones and dealing with clients for their appointments, you can observe Ken and me as we work." My heart skips a beat at the thought of starting my training. "We'll explain what we're doing while you observe and if you have questions, be sure to ask them. Remember, there is no such thing as a stupid question." He raises his dark brows and I nod. "You can have your phone with you, but I don't want to see you scrolling social media. There's always something that needs to be done around here."

"Yes, boss!" I salute him, to lighten the mood. His eyes widen slightly and his mouth twitches, almost like he's trying to hold back a smile.

Pushing to stand, he grabs his coffee and steps from behind his desk. "All right. I'll show you where everything is and grab Jenna's key for you." I follow him out of his office and across the hall to a small storeroom that's not much bigger than a utility closet, forcing our bodies to touch, sending scorching heat radiating through me. Oblivious to my reaction—which I work to squash so I can concentrate—he points to the various items as he explains what each one is and when it's used. Then he waves his arm out toward the bathroom and shows me where I can store my purse safely.

When we head out into the open front area, I touch the leaves of the plants as I pass. "I love the greenery. It adds a touch of softness to the place."

"That's Ken. He loves having the plants here. You'll hear him talking to them throughout the day. He even has names for each one." He pushes his hair out of his eyes. "I can never remember which one is which, so don't feel too bad if you can't keep them straight either."

A giggle escapes me before I can contain it. "I can't imagine Ken talking to the plants. He looks more like he belongs in a motorcycle club."

His body tenses. "Yeah, well, appearances can be deceiving." A note of warning slides into his tone. "He's the sweetest dude you'll ever meet." He flicks the light switch and bathes the large room in light. "When you first come in, you'll need to turn on the lights, start the computer, and ensure we have everything we need to begin work. If you notice we're getting low on stock, we have a notepad in the drawer at reception. Just add anything to the list."

"Okay."

"Sorry, I'm late. Traffic was a bitch, and the bean needed an extra slice of peanut butter toast." I turn toward the woman's voice and come face to face with Jenna, the stunning woman I met on Thursday when I came in for the interview. She thought I was a college girl wanting a tattoo. Her lips spread when she finally looks up at me and Lincoln. "Hey, congrats on getting the job! Linc showed me your art. You are one talented lady." She wraps her arm around my shoulder and gives me a side hug as if we know each other well. "Morning, boss."

"Morning." He steps close to her, inspecting her from top to bottom with narrowed eyes. "How are you feeling, Jen?"

"Didn't get much sleep last night. All of my insides feel as though they're squashed behind my ribs, but I'm feeling good right now. I'll probably nap this afternoon." She pushes a multitude of gorgeous braids over her shoulder. "You ready to get started?"

"Absolutely. Show me all the things I need to know."

"All right, I'll leave you ladies to it." He looks directly at me. "When you're finished with Jenna, Ken will show you how to set up our stations." Without waiting for a response, he spins on his heel and stalks to the front door to unlock it.

Jenna turns on the computer and while we wait for it to load, she explains what a typical flow will look like. "People may walk in or phone to make an appointment. The first appointment is a sit down with an artist while the client discusses what they would like. You may do a couple of quick sketches to confirm that you're both on the same page. You'll also need to do a tracing of the area where they want the tattoo so you have measurements as well as any scars, moles, or birthmarks you need to work with or around." She shows me the booking and payment system—explaining how each step of the workflow fits and how it looks in the program—which is similar to the one I've been using at *Beyond the Fringe* but different from the program *artWORX* used, but it's easy enough to pick up.

Ken breezes in with a watering can. "Morning, ladies."

When I turn to say good morning back, Jenna stops me with a chuckle. She leans in and whispers, "He's talking to his plants."

My eyes widen. "Oh."

"He'll get to us in a sec." She holds three fingers up and mouths, "three … two … one."

"Morning, doll." He wraps his arm around Jenna and gives her a side hug. "How are you feeling?" His eyes trace her from head to toe with concern. I love how Lincoln and Ken check in with Jenna like she's more than an employee. They feel more like a family.

She chuckles and presses her hand on his protruding belly. "I'm great. Especially now that I've seen you."

His cheeks turn pink. "How's the bean?"

She rubs her stomach lovingly, her expression softening. "The bean's doing great."

"Awesome." Ken turns his attention to me. "How are you doing, doll?"

I smile brightly because I'm living the dream right now. "I'm great, thanks. Jenna's showing me the computer system and explaining how the appointments work."

"Good. If there's anything you forget, you can always ask me or Linc,"—I slide my eyes to Lincoln, something I can't seem to stop myself from doing—"so don't stress if you can't remember everything." *Well, that takes some of the pressure off.*

"Thanks, Ken."

He nods, then makes his way around the room, watering his plants, twisting the pots, and talking to them as he does. It's quite a sight. The bell over the door rings and when I look toward the sound, a stocky guy with arms covered in colorful tattoos enters. Jenna nudges me. "Let's see what you've got."

I nod and smile. "Good morning, welcome to *Fine Line.* How can I help you today?"

He grins at me as he leans on the counter. "You could give me your number, beautiful."

Jenna chuckles as Linc's voice booms from his station where he's setting up. "Cut it out, Daniel." Daniel chuckles and Linc steps forward to look at me. "He's here for his appointment with me. He thinks he's a ladies' man. Just ignore him."

"Aww, damn. Stomp on a man's ego, why don't ya?" He says to Linc with a cheeky grin and a wink at me before greeting my boss with a familiar handshake. They make their way over to Lincoln's station, leaving Jenna and me alone.

"Hmm, interesting," Jenna murmurs.

"What's interesting?"

She glances at me, then across to Lincoln. "He never stopped Daniel from hitting on me when I first started here."

I wave off her comment. "It's probably because Linc thinks I'm *so* young."—I roll my eyes.—"If you could call twenty-six young."

She chews her lip. "Nah, I don't think so. I was only eighteen." My eyes widen. *Oh.* She nods, raising a single perfectly shaped brow. "Yeah. Anyway, you can mark Daniel as arrived." She points to the screen to show me how to do it. "And when he's finished and you take his payment, the square will turn blue."

My time with Jenna flies by and she heads out to meet her husband for lunch. After Ken explains how to set up each station and I deal with a phone call, I head over to Linc to watch him work. His focus is locked on his client's muscular thigh as he shades the scales of an enormous dragon wrapped around Daniel's leg. Each scale looks as though it's glistening and I swear if I were to touch it, it would feel cool like a snake. The tiger-slash-woman tattoo on Lincoln's left forearm shifts with the movement of his muscles as he holds Daniel's flesh taut, the blue eyes following me as I watch.

"Look at how I maintain three points of contact, Sophie. I anchor my elbow on the table, touch Daniel's leg with my wrist, and anchor my little finger against the thumb I use to stretch his skin." I study each point of contact carefully. It looks easy enough, but I bet it takes practice to get it right. "This keeps my hand steady to ensure my lines are always perfectly straight. I use my fingers beneath the gun to float the needle and keep the depth consistent as I work so I don't go too shallow or too deep." He returns his focus to his work and I lose myself watching the mesmerizing action as ink that looks almost iridescent fills each scale, one by one. I glance up at Daniel's face, finding him relaxed to the point of bliss.

HAVING SOPHIE SITTING SO CLOSE AND HER EYES ON MY WORK, soaking in every detail, is testing my restraint. She's eager to learn everything she can and her thoughtful questions show she's intuitive enough to consider how the artwork will interact with the play of muscles and skin tone. When I glance up from my work, her brown eyes catch mine and it could be pure coincidence, but my heart skitters. Her excitement about something that has become commonplace for me is tangible and I'm feeding off of it, making the scales I'm working on seem almost real.

I always do my best work because the client deserves my best every single time. They have to wear my art and I take pride in making each piece better than the last; but with her eyes on me, I'm pushing myself to the next level.

I blot the final spot and push away from the table, stretching out my back and neck. I need to practice taking regular breaks instead of getting lost in the work for hours on end. I never had a problem with aches and pains when I was younger, but getting older is a bitch now I'm closer to forty than thirty. It even takes me longer to recover from a fight, and that pisses me off because I know my time as a fighter is coming to an end. I'll have to work out a different way to raise money for the charity I support.

Daniel hops off the table, heads for the mirror, and twists his leg this way and that. "Man, this is fucking awesome."

"I'm glad you like it." I explain the aftercare for the new artwork to Sophie as I work. Daniel's a return customer, so he knows exactly what he needs to do over the next days and weeks.

The bell over the door rings and Sophie heads to the reception desk to greet the next client. While I clean up, she takes Daniel's payment and guides Natasha to the round table where we meet with clients to discuss their needs. I'm impressed at how well she's managing the front desk duties without a hitch. She said she was a fast learner and I don't think she was overselling herself.

"Sophie, how about you bring your sketchpad with you and sit in on our chat? Natasha is here to discuss a new tattoo she'd like. This would be a great opportunity to learn this part of the process and I wouldn't mind seeing you draw up some sketches."

Her eyes widen, and she bites her bottom lip. "Really? You think I can do that?"

"We'll see. But I'm confident you can handle drawing the sketches. Your line work is fantastic."

"Thank you." Her cheeks pinken and she drops her warm gaze from mine as she grabs her sketchpad to follow me to the table where Natasha is flipping through one of our design books.

I hold out my hand as I reach the table. "Hi, Natasha. I'm Lincoln and this is Sophie. This is Sophie's first day, so I hope you don't mind if she sits in."

She stands, taking my hand with a soft smile. "Hi, Lincoln. Sophie. I don't mind at all."

"Hi, Natasha. Thank you," Sophie says as we all sit.

"Tell us a little about what you're looking for," I say and nod toward Sophie's sketchpad. "We'll draw up some rough ideas from your thoughts."

Natasha swallows and licks her lips. "I heard you specialize in tattooing women who have had a mastectomy."

I nod. "I do. How far post-op are you?"

"Two years. I thought I could live with my new breasts, but every time I look in the mirror, all I see is what I've lost. I want to look at my body and love it again." She twists her fingers together. "It's affecting me *and* my marriage."

"Well, you've come to the right place. Do you have anything in mind?"

She shrugs. "This might sound silly, but I want something feminine and dainty. Beautiful." Out of the corner of my eye, I see Sophie drawing some swirly design on her pad. The lines are delicate and feminine, like a fine lace. It's exactly what Natasha is describing. "I hate that all I see are my scars and missing nipples."

I point to the sketchpad. "Something like this?"

Sophie's pencil doesn't stop as she adds more detail, more swirls, more lines. Natasha gasps, bringing her hand up to her chest and I glance at Sophie's face to see if she's noticed her reaction, but she's so far in the zone that I don't think she's even aware of anything happening around her right now.

"Oh my gosh, it's beautiful." She looks up at me, then back at the design. "Sophie, it's perfect."

At the sound of her name, Sophie looks up as if coming out of a daze. "Huh?"

I nudge Sophie's arm. "Natasha loves it."

"Really? I can do other designs for you."

"It's gorgeous. I don't need to see another design." Natasha points to the page. "This is the one I want."

Sophie's smile is instant and her shoulders straighten.

"Thank you. I'm so glad you like it. I can change any part of it and I'm sure we'll need to modify it to shape around your breasts properly. I imagine the design cupping your breasts like a bra would."

Natasha nods as her lips spread. "Perfect."

Ken wanders over to look at the design and his eyes widen when they land on Sophie's sketchpad. "Your lines are beautifully delicate, doll. This is a stunning piece."

She tips her head back to smile at him. "Thanks, Ken. That means a lot coming from someone as talented as you."

"All right. If this is the design you'd like, we need to take some measurements so Sophie can draw it properly. Do you mind following me over to the far table and we can drag the curtain around for privacy?"

"Sure."

Sophie, Natasha, and I head to the last table and I drag the curtain around. Natasha removes her shirt and bra and I trace the area we'll be working with, ensuring I mark the scars so Sophie can cover them effectively with lines, explaining each step. "Okay. Let's see when we can book you in. We'll leave you to dress. Please join us at reception when you're ready."

Sophie's almost giddy when we reach the reception desk. "I can't believe she liked my design straight up."

"I can. It's a stunning piece. You listened to what she wanted and delivered exactly what she asked for. You did a great job at listening to the client's request."

She ducks her head as pink paints her cheeks, again. When Natasha joins us, I talk Sophie through the booking system, particularly how to calculate the time a tattoo like this should take, and we look for a time slot that will allow enough time as well as fit in with Natasha's schedule. "All right, we'll see you in four weeks."

"How much will it cost?"

"We don't charge for mastectomy tattoos here."

Both Natasha and Sophie's eyes widen. "Really?"

"Yeah." I rub the back of my neck. "My mom survived breast cancer, so this is something I do to honor her victory."

Natasha blinks and her hand rises to cover her chest. "Oh, wow." Her eyes grow shiny. "Thank you so much."

I nod. I don't make a big deal out of doing what I do because it isn't a big deal to me in the scheme of things. But I know it's a big deal to the men and women who come here for tattoos to cover their battle scars. "You're welcome. See you when you come in."

"I can't wait. Thank you so much. I can't wait to show my husband once it's finished." Natasha walks out of the studio looking much lighter and freer than she did when she walked in. She'll have even more confidence the next time she walks out that door, and that's something that fills me with pride.

Sophie breaks me from my thoughts when she rests her hand on my arm, singeing my flesh. "You do all mastectomy tattoos for free?" I nod. "That's an incredible gift, Lincoln." She bites her bottom lip, then adds, "Sorry about your mom," she murmurs.

I shrug. "I guess I got to see first-hand the impact of losing breasts has on a woman. Even though she survived, it took a toll on her emotionally and mentally."

Sophie sighs and when I glance down at her, I can't read her expression, but I want to check in with her. "How did that appointment feel for you?"

"So good. Did you see how excited she was? That tattoo is going to change her life. It's going to make her feel comfortable in her skin again. That's a remarkable thing to do for someone."

And that's exactly the vibe I want from my employees and why I gave Sophie the job. "I did. I think you're going to fit in nicely." I hold out my hand to her and she slides hers into it cautiously. "Welcome to the team." I know I already welcomed her, but I feel deep down that she's going to be an incredible asset to *Fine Line*.

Her shoulders drop from around her ears and her grin spreads wide. "Thank you. I promise you won't be sorry."

Now to keep the relationship between us professional because every time I'm near the woman, I want to erase the space between us and do filthy things to her.

CHAPTER 7

—lincoln—

I use my forearm to wipe the sweat from my forehead, pushing my damn hair out of my eyes. I need to book a damn haircut. I move side to side and watch the ball intently, ensuring I'm ready if it comes anywhere near the goal I'm defending. It heads my way, so I move off the goal line, but Aaron intercepts it and kicks it back the other way. These Monday night soccer games are meant to be a fun way to get some exercise, but I'll be damned if I let a ball get past me. I'd never hear the end of it.

The final whistle blows, and the game is a draw at zero all. There's plenty of back-slapping to go around as we make our way off the field. I'm not too proud to say I was relieved to be in goals tonight because I didn't feel up to running around. Sleep's been almost impossible to come by the last two weeks, thanks to the woman who magically slips into my mind at the most inconvenient times.

I chuckle as a pregnant Molly wraps her arms around Max and he hoists her up by her ass so she can wrap her legs around him. Finn also has Harry in his arms before he clears the field. It used to be just the boys, but that all changed when Max hired Molly and subsequently fell in love with her. Who could blame him, she's a knockout and the sweetest woman I've ever met … *until Sophie*—now *she's* a sweetheart hiding beneath all that black eyeliner, painted lips, and messy hair—then Finn went and fell in love with the literal girl next door. I huff out a chuckle under my breath and collect my stuff from the sidelines.

"Beer and pizza?" Finn calls to everyone.

I raise my arm to respond. "Sure. See you in a few."

Aaron catches up to me beside my car. "Thanks for the ride tonight."

"Makes sense to share a ride," I tell him as I toss my bag onto the back seat.

"Yeah, well, it doesn't always work out between our schedules." True. Considering we live together, you would think we see each other all the time, but our schedules rarely align.

We climb in and make our way to *Brady's Pub*. Finn always supplies pizza after our Monday night games; we just need to buy our drinks. "You seemed to move okay tonight. How's the knee?"

He squeezes it. "Pretty good. I was careful, though. No point in making it worse. I need to run the café."

I tap my fingers on the dash. "Better to be safe than sorry when your livelihood's at stake."

We arrive at Finn's bar and climb into a booth with Max, Finn, and their ladies. They already have drinks, and Max pushes a glass toward each of us. "You can buy the next round."

I take a long gulp and raise my glass to my friend. "Thanks, man, appreciate it."

We shoot the shit until our pizzas arrive, then the table falls silent as we dig in. Finn's crew makes some of the best pizzas I've tasted. He installed a proper pizza oven after he took over the pub from his dad.

"I need to go to the bathroom," Molly says as she climbs out of the booth. Max kisses her like she's leaving town for a month and when he turns back to us, he's wearing a satisfied expression. Lucky bastard.

"So … are you looking forward to being a dad?" Aaron asks Max.

His spine straightens, and a grin slides across his lips. "I can't fucking wait. I can't wait to hold our baby. To teach them how to play soccer and work on cars. Molly's going to be the best mom ever and I'm excited to watch her with our little one."

"What about keeping them safe? Don't you worry about something happening to them?" I ask.

He shrugs. "Well, yeah. We won't let anything happen to them."

"But you can't guarantee that," I snap. I learned the hard way; that's why kids aren't in my plans.

"No, but we can do our best and not put them in a situation that would be dangerous." His eyes narrow at me as his brows dip low over his hazel eyes and guilt makes my stomach roll. *Is that what I did?* "What is this about, Linc?"

I shrug it off. "It's just difficult to keep kids safe all the time. I wanna make sure you guys have thought about that."

He nods slowly, as if he's rolling over my words in his head. "We'll work it out, Linc. I know Molly and I will do our best." *Yeah, but sometimes our best isn't enough.* "Our kids will be our priority and we won't let our guard down. I promise." His words ease something inside me. A deep worry that I've always carried with me since I was seven.

I blow the hair out of my face for the millionth time and Sophie chuckles. "I can make an appointment for you at *Beyond the Fringe* if you like."

I stop my gun, remove it from the client's skin, and peer up at her. "Yeah?"

She raises and drops one shoulder. "I'm always happy to help however I can." She's already shown us that, but organizing a haircut isn't part of her duties; she's not my personal assistant. "I can text Hope, my old manager."

"Is she any good?"

She nods sharply. "One of the best. She specializes in curly and wavy hair."

"Well, yeah, thanks. I'd appreciate it."

I finish up with my client and explain the aftercare procedure carefully. He nods a lot, but I don't trust he's going to take it seriously. "It's important that you follow these instructions properly, man." I shove my finger down on the aftercare pamphlet.

"Yeah, man. No problem-o." He tips his chin up at me, raps his knuckles on the counter, and heads out the door, leaving the pamphlet behind.

Sophie looks at me with raised brows. "What are the chances he's gonna end up with an infection and will need to come back?"

"Pretty high."

Sophie heads over to my station to sanitize the area, and I head to the office to print the design for Aaron. He's been wanting something for a while and this geometric leg sleeve is going to look fantastic.

Sophie walks in, stopping right beside me, holding up her phone. "Hope can fit you in first thing in the morning." She covers the receiver. "She had a last-minute cancellation. I'd grab it if I were you, because she's always fully booked."

"Okay, yeah. I'll take it. Thanks."

She grins, then turns her back to me and my eyes drop to admire her round ass, which is right there in my face and my hands itch to touch it, caress it, grab it.

"Oh, I love it here. It's exactly where I'm meant to be. Yeah, my boss is amazing." My heart expands with pride at the happiness in her tone. "Thanks, Hope, I'll see you tomorrow." I frown as she disconnects the call. "You're booked in for eight."

Leaning her hip against my desk, her coconut scent surrounds me. I'm never going to be able to enjoy coconut without associating it with Sophie. "Thanks. Are you getting a haircut too?"

She tilts her head to the side. "No. I thought I'd come with you so I can introduce you."

That would mean we'll spend time together outside of work, which could be dangerous for me. She already has me in a twist and I'm not sure if it would be such a good idea. "You don't have to go to any trouble. Just shoot me the address."

She waves her hand in the air. "It's no trouble. It'll be great to see Hope." Her eyes trace my face carefully and her delicate eyebrows lower. *Damn.* "Unless you don't want me there," she says slowly, a little hurt coloring her tone.

"Linc!" Ken barges into the office, holding his phone over his head. "Jenna had her baby! It's a girl!"

"Oh, that's great news," Sophie says brightly as she takes a step away from me. "Did she say what her name is?"

"Olivia Jayne."

She grins as if she's known Jenna for years and they're best friends. "Such a pretty name." She glances at me. "Isn't it a great name?"

Ken's eyes flick between me and Sophie with interest.

"Yeah, it is," I agree, then turn back to Ken. "Are they okay?"

Ken's eyes catalog my features and he nods. He knows what

I'm asking. "Yeah. She didn't say anything was wrong, so I would assume they're both doing okay."

The muscles across my shoulders relax and I breathe a sigh of relief. "Was Dean there for the delivery?"

He shrugs. "Her message didn't say."

"I'll call her later."

The bell for the front door rings and Sophie leaves the office. Ken leans against the doorjamb. "What was going on in here?"

I turn my attention back to my desk. "Sophie booked me in for a haircut at her old salon."

"Was that all that was happening because I felt some tension in here when I walked in?" A tinge of concern in his tone.

"Yep."

He studies me closely and I studiously concentrate on my task, avoiding eye contact with him. He knows me too well. I started my apprenticeship here with him when I was in my late teens and eventually bought the studio from him when he no longer wanted the strife of operating a business. He huffs but leaves me to my muddled thoughts.

—sophie—

I SUCK IN A LUNGFUL OF AIR TO ERASE LINCOLN'S SEXY CEDAR scent from my lungs as I leave the office and head to the front desk.

He's my boss. He's my boss. He's my boss. I repeat the mantra, to remind myself of our relationship.

I don't know why I want to go with him to his appointment. I have a ton of stuff I need to do before work tomorrow. Maybe I shouldn't go; it's not like he was keen on the idea. His obvious rejection reminded me we're nothing more than work colleagues. We're not friends who hang out outside of work hours. I can catch up with Hope another time.

I shake off my confusion, paste on a smile, and greet the gentleman standing at the counter. When he tells me he's here for his appointment for his leg sleeve, I lead him to Linc's station, which is already prepared, and begin shaving his lower leg.

Linc meets us there and pulls Aaron into a familiar man hug, then turns to me. "Sophie, this is my best friend and roommate. Aaron, this is Sophie."

Aaron raises his eyebrows at Lincoln and turns to me with

a wicked grin. "Great to meet you, Sophie." He thumbs over his shoulder. "Is this guy behaving?"

I chuckle, catching Linc's eyes over his friend's shoulder. "He's a great boss."

"Good to hear. You let me know if anything changes." He winks at me.

Linc pushes his shoulder,—"She won't need to. I'm a fucking exceptional boss."—then shoves him back into the chair and shows Aaron the final design for his tattoo while I complete my task. Once I'm finished, I clean up the mess and make myself scarce.

I need to keep my distance until I can work out why I feel the need to go to his appointment with him. My first thought is that I'm being a good friend. He doesn't know Hope, so it makes sense for me to be there.

When I dig deeper, I know I'm lying to myself. I have a lot of respect for Lincoln. He's wicked talented, and he's been patient as he teaches me the ins and outs of becoming a proficient tattoo artist. The more time I spend with him, the more my respect grows. But that's not the only thing that grows. I'm insanely attracted to the man. Where I once thought he was gruff and angry, he's actually sweet and caring. Every morning, he has a cup of coffee waiting for me at the front desk and he always makes sure I take my breaks. His sheer masculinity calls to my most feminine side, and his appeal becomes more potent every day as I spend more time with him.

Sometimes I sense the attraction goes both ways, which is surprising considering he made a big deal about how young I looked. I admit I don't know him outside of work, only that he fights, which is a red flag for me. I'm not sure I could bring him around James, but I quickly shake the thought out of my head because I'm getting ahead of myself.

I startle when a hand lands on my lower back and I spin around, whacking the person behind me with the dustpan, sending Aaron's leg hair everywhere. "Sorry." I drop to my knees to clean up the mess behind the reception desk, but Lincoln captures my elbow, stopping me.

"Completely my fault." His eyes catch on my mouth and pause there. *See.* When he does that, it seems like he's attracted to me. I drop my eyes to the center of his chest, tuck my loose hair behind my ear, and do my best not to lick my lips, which suddenly feel parched. He dips at the knees, catches my chin with his knuckle, and lifts my head so I have to look him in the eye. *We're having a moment, right? It isn't my imagination.* After a pause, he drops his hand and steps away from me. "Since you've already done the initial prep, would you like to position the stencil? I'll guide you through it to make sure it's lined up correctly. I've already asked Aaron, and he's okay with it."

My confusion is forgotten and my grin is instantly obnoxious. "Absolutely."

"Okay. Wash your hands and meet me at my station."

My hands shake with anticipation as I put on a fresh pair of gloves. I've done this on fake skin, but this is the first time on a real person and I want to get it just right. I want to make Lincoln proud of me, especially in front of his friend. I want to show him he didn't make a mistake when he hired me.

Linc asks Aaron to stand on the small platform he has on hand and passes the skin marker to me in my kneeled position. "Okay, look at Aaron's knee, and let's measure the central point." I do as he says and look up to him for confirmation before I mark the spot. A mistake on my part, because my eyes land directly on his crotch, which has an impressive bulge behind the zipper. I swallow and shift my eyes up to his face, hoping he didn't notice. "Yep, that looks good. Mark it." I do as he says. "Now use your fingers to feel your way down his shin until you get to his ankle. Where do you think the central point is?"

I concentrate hard, ensuring I maintain the line along his bone. "Here?"

"Yep. Good girl. Mark it." Tingles erupt across my body at his praise. *Geez, girl, keep yourself in check.*

He passes me the stencil. "See how I've already marked the center here at the top and bottom, line the points up, and let's see how it sits."

I do as he says, and he tells me to draw a mark across the stencil and onto Aaron's leg to make it easier to find the right position once we're ready to apply it. Linc passes the stencil stuff and I shake it like Ken taught me, then rub the white cream uniformly over the area for the tattoo. Once it's tacky to the touch, I realign the marks I made and press the stencil evenly onto Aaron's shin. I peel it off slowly and am happy to see the stencil pattern is perfect and exhale a long breath.

"You did a good job. Now we'll wait ten to fifteen minutes and I can start inking the design. Thanks, Soph."

I sit and observe Linc as he inks the geometric design to the front of Aaron's lower leg. This tattoo is being done in two sections because it's a sizable piece. I completely forget about my need to put distance between us and get lost in the mesmerizing strokes of Linc's gun.

"Soph?" I spin in my seat toward Ken.

"Yeah."

He tips his head toward the reception desk and the sound of the phone ringing. "You wanna get that?"

Flustered, I jump to my feet. "Yeah, sure."

I answer the call and tell the young woman that we have a three-month wait list which she isn't happy about, but I take her information and book an initial appointment for her. I know the guys are falling behind with taking new bookings because I'm still in training and a pang of guilt makes itself known in my gut. If Linc had hired the other applicant, he wouldn't have had to delay these appointments, but then I wouldn't be living my dream. Ken motions for me to come over to him, so I head in his direction.

"Everything okay?" I look at him in confusion. "The phone was ringing for a while and you didn't notice."

Shit! "Uh, yeah. Everything's okay. Sorry, I didn't hear the phone. I was so caught up watching Lincoln work I must have zoned out." Ken nods and returns to the back tattoo he's working on—a gorgeous angel wearing a bloodied cape and wielding a giant sword above her head with two hands. The expression on her face is fierce and I can feel her power emanating from the image. I decide to take a break from watching Lincoln and pull up the spare chair to watch Ken work for a while. "This is stunning work, Ken."

He grins but doesn't take his eyes off his work. "Thanks, doll."

I spin my fork around in my pasta and raise it to my mouth.

"We were going to stop by and say *hello* after school today, but I had a plot bunny I needed to get down on paper. It came to me as I was collecting James from the bus stop and I was worried I'd forget. Maybe we'll stop by another day."

The pasta goes down the wrong pipe and I choke—coughing and spluttering so much I can't catch my breath. James quickly jumps from his seat and pats my back while Dad pushes my glass of water closer—*Shit! What if they'd turned up? My secret would be out and Dad would demand that I quit the most perfect job in the world*—and I finally get myself under control to take a sip.

"You okay, sweetie?" Dad studies me like he's waiting for me to collapse.

I clear my throat and nod. "Yeah, the pasta went down the

wrong pipe." I take a long drink and swallow. "I don't think it's a good idea for you to visit me at work yet. I haven't even been there a month and the boss can be grouchy about visitors during work hours." I have no idea if that's true.

Creases form between Dad's brows. "I hope he's not grouchy with you. You don't deserve that sort of treatment. Don't put up with that." He jabs his fork in my direction.

"I haven't given him a reason to be grumpy yet and I intend to keep it that way." I take another bite of my pasta and swallow. "I would appreciate it if you waited a little longer before you visit."

He nods. "Okay. We can do that, can't we, James?"

"Sure can." He pushes away from the table to take his empty plate to the sink. "Can we have ice cream tonight? I ate all of my dinner."

I smile at him. "Have you done all of your homework?" Since I get home at dinner time now, I have to check that he's doing what he should.

He nods his head like a bobble doll. "I have. I even did some extra math, didn't I, Grandad?"

Dad smiles, his gaze full of pride. "You sure did."

"All right. Once we clean up the dishes, I'll fix you an ice cream cone."

He cheers as he returns to the table and I tell them all about Jenna having her baby girl today.

"A baby is such a beautiful blessing. I'll say a prayer for them tonight before bed."

I smile softly. "That's very kind of you, Dad."

He's never wavered from his faith, even though he lost the love of his life and the use of his legs in a train wreck. From what I've researched about it, the accident was horrific. I was only two at the time; too young to remember Mom or the tragedy of losing her. Dad had a meeting across town with a prospective publisher, so we caught the train with plans to enjoy lunch afterward. During the ride home, a truck driver crossed the track, causing the train to derail. That day, five people, including Mom, lost their lives, and many others, including Dad, sustained severe injuries. I have a scar that runs from my breastbone to beneath my breasts, but no memory of the event. I only know of it from the few times Dad's spoken about it and news articles I've seen online.

Before I climb into bed, I grab my phone and text Lincoln the address of *Beyond the Fringe*. I think it's best if I keep my distance. No point making things harder for myself.

CHAPTER 9

—lincoln—

I STEP ONTO THE PORCH, MY EYES LINGERING ON THE SPOT where my sister last sat all those years ago. I hate that Mom still lives here, but she refuses to move in case Elizabeth somehow finds her way back to us. I knock once and jam my key in the lock, then open the front door. "Hi, Mom!" I call as I place the cake I brought on the table.

"In here!" Her voice comes from the back of the house, and I know exactly where I'll find her before I take my next step. I fucking loathe it when she's in there, but it's the same thing every year on my sister's birthday. She spends the day cleaning it from top to bottom, washing all of my sister's little girl clothes, the bedding … even the damn curtains.

Standing on the threshold of the doorway, I dig my hands deep into my pockets and refuse to take another step. I trace the jungle-inspired walls and decor with my eyes. It's the perfect room for a three-year-old girl who was crazy about tigers. A little girl who hasn't been around for over thirty years. Bile rises from my gut and I swallow quickly, trying to stop its pathway up my throat. "Mom, I brought cake. Let's have a slice." I need to get her out of this room before I throw up.

She spins around to face me, wiping beneath her eyes. "Elizabeth is thirty-five today."

I nod and cross the threshold as I shove my feelings aside to comfort her, as I've always done. Wrapping my arm around her shoulder, I tug her close. "Yeah, Mom. That's why I brought cake."

Her lips rise shakily and she looks up at me with glassy eyes. "Okay."

Leaning her weight into me, I guide her to the kitchen so she can sit. I quickly collect the cake I left at the front door and grab two cups and plates down from the cupboard, then make our drinks as I ruminate over what to say. Mom's always struggled on Beth's birthday and the day she went missing.

The day our world fell apart.

The day someone stole my baby sister from us.

An event that was entirely my fault.

My heart falters and my gut churns, but I force the discomfort away—I don't deserve comfort for *my* pain, so I ignore it—and support Mom in her grief. Her watery gaze follows me as I prepare two slices of cake and two cups of coffee.

"How are you doing, Linc?"

I carry everything to the table and take a seat as I shrug. "Same old. Nothing much changes ... work, Monday night soccer, gym, home." I make the mistake of looking at her instead of concentrating on my piece of cake as planned. Her dull blue eyes study me like she can uncover all of my secrets.

"You know what I'm asking. Don't avoid the question," she pushes. Instead of answering, I shove a forkful of cake into my mouth to bide my time. She sighs loudly. "I wish you'd talk to me."

I chew and swallow. "There's nothing to talk about, Mom. I promise I'm doing okay." I take a drink. "It's been a long time."

"I know ... Lord, I know. But pain is pain. It may ease a

little, but it never goes away. We just learn to live around it."
Oof. I feel that on so many levels. We're both quiet, lost in our thoughts for a few minutes, and I cherish the silence. "I thought I saw her the other day," Mom murmurs.

I snap my head toward her. In my mind's eye, Beth's still three and even though we don't know if she's still alive, I struggle to picture what she might look like as a grown woman. "What?"

She shakes her head, and a tear drops from her lashes. "It was probably my imagination. But the woman had our blue eyes, and she looked about the right age."

Hope rises swiftly, but I force it away. There have been so many false alarms over the years. "Mom, you know that *if* she is still alive—and that's a huge *if*—someone would have taken her far away from here."

She nods, but I see the hope in her eyes and it kills me. "I know. But what *if* …"

"Mom," I chastise. Her lips tremble and I climb to my feet to pull her into my embrace, where she buries her face in my chest. "Don't keep doing this. It's too painful."

She nods. "I know. I just … I just can't help it. I want her to be alive and happy. Healthy and settled with her own family. I want a beautiful life for my baby girl."

I stroke her back. "I know, Mom. I want those things for her, too." It's better for both of us if we believe she's alive and doing well somewhere out there in the world instead of thinking about the alternative.

She pulls her head back and looks up at me. "Do you think I'm a grandma?"

I smile the best I can. "I'm sure you are. If anyone deserves to be blessed with grandkids, it's you."

She pushes away from me and returns to her seat. "You could give me some."

"Mom. Really? That's low." She may as well have plunged a butcher's knife through the muscle in my chest.

She drops her gaze to the table and shrugs. "You can't blame me for trying. I'm not getting any younger, Lincoln."

"You know how I feel about kids. It's too damn hard to keep them safe. I can't take that sort of risk." *I won't.* It would literally kill me if something happened to them.

Her eyes glisten and we fall quiet again. If only I'd brought Beth inside with me when she grazed her knee instead of racing inside to get a Band-Aid. She would still be here to celebrate her birthday with us.

I lay into the bag with several punches and finish with a kick to the imaginary obliques. Sweat coats my skin and my muscles ache, but I needed to fucking punch something this afternoon. I drove straight here from Mom's and was grateful the space I needed was vacant. My lungs heave, filling with oxygen, but I raise my hands and start the routine over. Maybe if I tire myself out enough, I'll be able to sleep tonight.

"Looking good up there, Linc!" Mike shouts. I drop my hands and rest them on my hips as I turn toward him.

"Thanks."

He tips his head toward the bag I was demolishing. "You ready for a fight this Thursday? Your name came out of the pool."

I wipe my forehead with my arm. "Yeah, sounds good, man." I step closer. "Who?"

He smirks. "You know I can't tell you that."

"Worth a try." I shrug and return his smirk.

"Yeah, not gonna happen." He taps the rope along the side of the mat. "See ya Thursday night."

I say goodbye to his retreating back and decide to call it a day. Grabbing my bag, I head to my car—I need a shower and a beer.

And that's where Aaron finds me—on our back porch, feet resting on the railing, and a beer to my lips.

He sits beside me with his beer. We're both silent as we watch the sun sink into the horizon, painting the sky with slashes of rose and peach. "You okay?" he asks without taking his eyes from the view.

I can be honest with Aaron. He's been my best friend since kindergarten. He knows *everything*. He was there to drag me out of bars after a fight. He held me as I cried until I passed out drunk. He *knows* the true impact losing my sister has had on me over the years—even before we were mature enough to understand. I've shared more of my burden with him than anyone, including Mom. Over the years, I've protected her from a lot of my pain. I'd be fucking ashamed for her to know even a quarter of what I've done. I take a long drink and shrug. "I've been better." I pick at the label on the bottle. "Mom was a mess, as usual."

"To be expected."

"I guess." I blow out an exhausted breath. "It's been a long time."

"Doesn't matter." He looks at me. "There isn't a time limit for this sort of thing. Especially since you guys don't have closure."

I swallow and decide to tell Aaron about a possible sighting. "Mom thinks she saw Beth, and it got her wondering if she has kids. Then she started on me about giving her grandkids."

He huffs out a laugh. "Only your mom would work out a way to use Beth's disappearance to pressure you about kids." He shakes his head and takes a sip of his drink. He's not a fan of my mother. "Do you think you'll ever change your mind about having kids one day if you meet the right woman?"

I shake my head. "Hell, no. I've had a front-row seat to the devastation caused when the worst possible scenario happens." We're both silent for a long while. "Do you think it's possible that Beth could be living here?" I whisper into the space between us.

He exhales a long breath. "I dunno, man. It seems unlikely, but stranger things have happened." He climbs to his feet. "You want another?"

I tip up my bottle and drink the last of it. "Sure. Thanks."

He returns a few moments later with two focaccias from his café and two fresh beers like the best friend he is.

—sophie—

Using the iPad to design a tattoo has been a learning curve, but I love the way I can shape the lines perfectly with a simple stroke as opposed to sketching it out on paper. I can't wait to watch Linc ink this piece onto Natasha's breasts. Glancing out of the front window to the street, I spot Lincoln returning with his lunch—something I normally go out to get for him, but he understood I needed to tweak this design. I want it to be perfect. Dropping my eyes back to my work, I ensure the swirl that will sweep up over the area where there should be a nipple is delicate, yet detailed enough to disguise the missing areola.

I'm acutely aware of every shift of Lincoln's body as he stands close and his scent surrounds me, sending unfamiliar signals firing through my synapses. "That looks spectacular. It's going to cup her breasts like the best lacy bra money can buy."

Warmth fills my body and my lips tip up at his praise, but it's more his tone of approval that makes me happy. Anyone can love a piece of art, but it's something else to have an artist you admire think your work is *spectacular*. It means so much more. I tip my head back and almost gasp at the appreciation in his blue gaze as he studies the artwork on the iPad. "Thank you. I want it to be perfect. She's already been through so much; she deserves to have beautiful work on her body."

He raises his gaze to mine. "It will be. You've done an awesome job. I can't wait to ink it." He swallows and places an iced latte on the reception desk next to me. "Are you still okay to stay late so you can see how I do it?"

I point to the drink. "Thanks for this." He's always doing sweet things for me, such a turnaround from the man who seemed unhappy to hire me. "Yeah, of course." I drop my head back to the device to hide my guilt. I told Dad I was going out with the girls from *Beyond the Fringe* because I couldn't think of a reason I'd need to work late in the job he *thinks* I have. He thought it was strange to go out on a Tuesday night, but still gave me his blessing. God. The lies keep stacking up. I'm going to need to write notes on my calendar soon. "I wouldn't want to miss seeing my first design being inked. I can't wait to see it finished."

The sun is sinking below the buildings, creating glittering reflections on the windows when Natasha walks through the door with a man at her side. I'm giddy at the thought of what's about to happen. My very first design is going to be on her skin forever. *Forever!* "Hi, Natasha."

"Hi, Sophie." She gestures toward the man beside her. "This is my hubby, Jacob."

"Hi, Jacob. Welcome to *Fine Line*."

He looks around, taking everything in. "Thanks. This place is not what I was expecting." He drops his gaze to his wife. "You were right. It has a great vibe."

Lincoln steps through the door from the back area and Natasha turns toward him, her grin huge. She grabs Jacob's arm and drags him forward with her. "Jacob, this is Lincoln. He's doing my tattoo."

Lincoln's smile transforms his face from broody to friendly

in an instant as he holds out his hand. "Hey, Jacob. Good to meet you, man." He looks down at Natasha. "I'm glad you brought someone for support."

"Good to meet you, too. I wasn't about to let her go through this on her own. I've been with her every step of the way. When she decided she needed to do this, I wanted to support her."

They talk for a few minutes, and then Lincoln leads them to his station. We've already discussed that I'll do the prep and position the stencil under his guidance if Natasha's happy to let me do that much. We ask for her permission, which she happily grants and I set about following the protocols to get her ready for her tattoo. My hands shake slightly as I shave her breasts to ensure the area is completely smooth. I've done a fair bit of shaving over the last few weeks, but it's strange to shave a woman's boobs. I wonder how Jacob feels having a man tattoo his wife's breasts.

With the shaving complete, I place the design where I want it and Lincoln hands me the marker so I can ensure I get it exactly right when I use the stencil stuff to transfer the design to her skin. He's not walking me through this step-by-step this time, understanding that I already know exactly where I want the tattoo to sit.

"Take your time, Soph. You've put a lot of time into the artwork; the positioning must be exactly how you envisioned," Lincoln quietly encourages.

I draw in a deep breath and relax my shoulders, then look up at Natasha. "Thanks for your patience. I want this to be perfect for you."

She smiles kindly. "It will be."

Her faith in me bolsters my confidence and with steady hands I place the design, ensuring the swirls sit perfectly where her nipples should be as the lacy outer design cups the shape of her breasts like a bra. When I finally peel the design away, I gasp at the sight of *my* artwork on her skin. Goosebumps race across my body, and a shiver makes its way up my spine.

When I glance up at Lincoln, his smile is warm, and his eyes are full of pride. "It's perfect." He glances up at Jacob. "What do you think?"

He shakes his head in wonder. "It's beautiful. It's exactly what I imagined when Tash told me about the design you sketched at her first appointment."

I'm glad he likes it, but the only person who truly counts is Natasha. I hold a mirror in front of her and study her face. Her eyes glisten and she covers her mouth with one hand. I watch as her eyes trace every part of her breasts. "This is incredible." She looks at me. "I'm so honored to be the first person to wear your beautiful art."

My stomach flips, my heart expands, and before I know what I'm doing, I've pushed into her and wrapped her in a loose hug so I don't rub the stencil from her boobs. She immediately returns my embrace and whispers *thank you* into my ear, and I realize this is going to be the best part of the job. Having my designs on someone else's body will be amazing, but knowing that my design makes them feel better about themselves is going to top that for me. And even though I've lied to my father about my job, I've finally found where I'm meant to be.

Ken wanders around the studio, saying goodnight to his plants before calling out goodnight to us. I'm not usually here this late, so I'm unfamiliar with his routine, but his love for his plants stretches my lips. Natasha smiles too.

The studio is silent except for the buzz of Lincoln's gun and the low murmur of Natasha and Jacob's conversation. Now and then, Lincoln explains his technique as he works over a scarred area of skin and I pay close attention to everything he says and does. I remember how it felt to have the tattoo gun on my scars and I glance up at Natasha's face to check she's okay.

Unsure how much time has passed, I adjust my position in my chair, stretching out my neck as Lincoln turns off his gun and wipes the area he was working on. "Finished." He rolls back, peeling his gloves off as he studies his work, then gestures to me. "Come back here and take a look."

I do as he says and gasp. Blinking quickly to prevent the tears burning my eyes from falling over my lashes, I shake my head. It looks gorgeous and her boobs look fantastic. The scarring is almost completely invisible to the eye and you wouldn't know that her nipples are missing. It's perfect. "You did such a great job, Linc," I tell him absently while admiring the design and the way it cups Natasha's breasts.

"It helps when I have an awesome design to work with." He grabs the mirror and holds it up for Natasha.

Her mouth falls open and tears rapidly fill her eyes, unable to be contained. Jacob wraps his arm around her and she buries her face in his chest for several minutes. He quietly strokes her hair and back while whispering to her. Her body trembles, but she slowly gets her emotions under control. When she pulls away from her husband, her eyes are red and puffy and embarrassment colors her features. "I'm so sorry. It's just that … it's so beautiful. I can honestly say that I don't think I'll be able to stop looking at my boobs now. I used to avoid looking in the mirror because I hated what I saw. You've made me love my body again. I don't know how to say thank you."

"You just did," Lincoln tells her.

Jacob thanks us too, and then Lincoln allows me to explain the aftercare. I refuse to take the money she tries to give me, even though she knows there's no charge. We share a last hug before I lock the door behind them. When I turn back to the room, Lincoln's nowhere to be seen, so I set about closing out the computer and cleaning up his station. The entire time I work, I ruminate over Natasha's reaction to her new tattoo, which has changed her view of herself, and I sniffle a little as I wipe my wet cheeks.

"That went well. Your design was perfect, and it looked fantastic. Once it's healed, it'll look even better than it did tonight." He freezes when he gets within a couple of feet of me and his dark brows drop low over his piercing eyes. "What's wrong?"

As much as I've tried to hold in my emotions, a sob breaks free and more tears burst forth. Embarrassed, I bury my face in my hands and try to temper my emotions. Lincoln's large hand slides into my hair, his hard body presses against mine, and he cradles me against his warmth. I drop my hands to grip his T-shirt on either side of his trim waist and mumble an apology into his chest, "I'm so-sorry. I don't understand what's come over me." Another sob breaks free without my permission and my cheeks flame with embarrassment.

Geez, girl, get a grip. He's gonna think you're a crazy woman.

His large hand strokes up and down my back in comfort, but that doesn't stop my traitorous body from responding to his touch. I press against him, soaking up his quiet support as my tears ebb. I don't know how I ever thought he was an angry man, because he's always been steady and patient with me.

"The first time you see your work on someone's skin can be emotional. And Natasha's response to it was … intense. I'm not surprised you're feeling the way you are."

I feel the vibration of his deep voice against my face as he speaks and, as embarrassed as I am, I can't resist looking at his face to check if he's as sincere as he sounds. The intensity etched in his handsome features steals my breath and my words.

His gaze traces my face carefully, then his hands cradle my head and his thumbs tenderly stroke the tears on my cheeks.

My lips part and the distance between us vanishes slowly as my heart gallops, making the blood in my veins thrum. I desperately want his lips on mine. I know it's wrong and inappropriate, but I find the man appealing on so many levels.

My nipples pebble against his hard body and I can't mistake what's happening below his belt. He scrunches his eyes closed, groans, and then his lips swipe mine with the softest of touches. So soft, I'm unsure if I imagined his touch.

"I shouldn't be doing this, but I'll be damned if I can resist any longer," he murmurs harshly. His lips brush mine with every word while his hot breath sends waves of goosebumps crashing over my skin and then our mouths connect with a touch so tender that it doesn't match the husky tone of his voice and the tenseness against my body.

He brushes his lips across mine, then sweeps his tongue across the seam, eliciting a sigh as I shudder. Pressing against him, I encourage him to deepen the kiss and he doesn't disappoint. His tongue delves inside my mouth with wicked strokes.

My breaths grow shallow as I return his kiss with enthusiasm. It's enough to kick the kiss up another notch and I'm quickly out of my depth as his fingers tighten in my hair, twisting it, and dragging my head back. He kisses me like he can't live another moment without tasting me, and I rock my body into him to eliminate any space between us.

A ragged groan rumbles from deep within his chest, vibrating against me and ratcheting up my need. No one has ever kissed me so wickedly before. I guess that's the difference between kissing a high school boy and a grown-ass man. He puts his whole body into it and I'm here for every second of this deliciousness.

Finding my courage, I release his T-shirt from my grip and slide my hands up his obliques, feeling the hard, defined muscles beneath my fingertips. His muscles twitch as I continue my exploration with more confidence, while his kiss grows more demanding. Scratching my fingernails across his back, I grin internally when another groan rumbles from him. His hands slide down, gripping my ass firmly, and he lifts me from my feet. Wrapping my legs around his slim hips, I grind down on the hardness confined in his black jeans.

CHAPTER 11

—lincoln—

SHE TASTES AS SWEET AS I THOUGHT SHE WOULD WITH A SIDE serving of inexperience, but that could be wishful thinking on my part. I'd love to believe I'm the first man she's ever kissed, but there's no way that could be a possibility, because the woman is a fucking knockout. Actually, I take that back. I don't want the responsibility of being her first anything, especially since it's happening here and not in a fancy hotel.

As much as I shouldn't be doing this with my employee, I also can't believe it's taken us this long for the tension between us to boil over. Each day spent working alongside her has tested my resolve to the point of no return. Now that I've tasted her mouth, I want to taste her everywhere.

With her delectable ass in my hands and her pussy grinding against my cock, I carry her toward the back office where we'll have more privacy. Our kiss doesn't slow and what she lacks in experience, she certainly makes up for with enthusiasm. Her hands make it to my hair and her harsh tugs send my pulse spiking. Reluctantly dragging my mouth from hers to draw in a breath, I place her on my clean desk.

The desk *she* keeps organized for me.

Because she's my employee.

Damn.

What the hell am I doing?

I take a giant step back, look up at the ceiling, and run my hand through my hair. When I finally drop my eyes to the woman sitting on my desk with her breasts heaving and eyes full of confusion, my cock begging for release and my blood pounding in my ears, I pause.

What the fuck am I doing?

I'm twelve years her senior.

And her boss.

This is wrong on so many levels.

So why does it feel so right?

More right than anything I've felt before.

"Linc?" Soph murmurs as she closes her legs self-consciously, making me feel like an asshole.

I pace the small office like a caged lion, darting my eyes back to her each time I pass her and noting her flushed cheeks, bright eyes, and puffy lips. *Fuck.* I step into her body, shoving my way between her thighs again, and cup her face—"I'm sorry."—then I slam my mouth down on hers. A startled gasp bursts out of her and I take advantage, spearing my tongue inside.

Our kiss is devastating.

She's devastating.

This woman has the power to destroy me.

Turn me to bone and ash.

But I don't stop. *I can't.*

I tangle my fingers in her silky hair and drag her head back so I can kiss my way down her sexy throat, just as I've imagined. The vibration of her moan tickles my lips, escalating my need for her. Sliding one hand down her lithe body, I slip my fingers beneath her silky shirt, and the heat of her flesh scorches me.

When I press my cock against her like an unrestrained teen, she answers by pushing her tits against me as I lightly glide my fingers up her ribs until I reach the silk of her bra.

Tearing my mouth from hers, I pull away to take a breath, trailing her stunning features with my eyes. She takes a moment to open hers, revealing their now-familiar warmth. Her messy hair makes my lips tip up on one side and her swollen lips call to me, so I press another softer kiss to them.

Dropping my fingers to the buttons of her shirt, I ask, "Can I take this off?"

I watch her throat move as she swallows. A note of nervousness touches her eyes, and as I'm about to call an end to everything, she nods slowly, bringing her fingers up to her buttons. "I can do it."

Pushing her hands out of the way, I unfasten the first button. "I want to." I lean in, press a kiss to her jaw near her ear, and whisper, "I want the pleasure of undressing you."

She inhales a sharp breath but drops her hands to the table and leans back, pushing her tits out. I barely hold back a groan at her explicit invitation. I study her closely as I unfasten each button; it's fucking torture not to drop my eyes to feast on her exposed breasts, but I do it—*pretty sure I deserve an award for my restraint.* When I undo the last button and slide the silky fabric from her shoulders, I allow myself to look at her and blow out a long stream of air at the vision before me. A lavender bra cups her perfect breasts, but it's the inked design—that can only be her artwork—that begins between her breasts and sweeps beneath them that steals my attention. It's beautifully delicate.

Releasing the front clasp of her bra, I push the fabric out of the way so I can trace the fine lines on her soft flesh, noting the raised tissue hidden within the design. "This is stunning. It has to be your artwork." I flick my eyes up to hers in time to see her nod as I continue to trace her flesh, noting the length of the hidden scar. "Can I ask about this?"

Her eyes widen slightly, but she nods. "I was a passenger on a train that derailed." Fuck! She raises and drops one shoulder, biting her bottom lip as her eyes slip away from mine and her chin dips a little. "My mom died and my dad lost the use of his legs. I got off lucky."

Lucky? Fucking hell. "I'm so fucking sorry, Soph." *What else can I say?*

"It's been a long time. I was only two when it happened."

"Still. You lost your mom. That's a fucking tragedy." She nods and I hate the melancholy that's filled the space between us. It has no place here, so I lean in and kiss her.

I kiss her like I've wanted to kiss her for weeks.

I soak up her taste and steal her breaths for my own.

I kiss her to replace a shitty moment with a hopefully better one.

I kiss her *because I can't fucking stop.*

I kiss my way across her jaw and down her slender throat. Further still, until my lips touch the delicate ink concealing her hurt and as I trace down one line of the Henna-inspired tattoo, an uncomfortable feeling rolls in my gut when I think about someone else touching her beautiful body. "Who did your tattoo?" I grit between my teeth.

"Barry at *artWORX.*"

I suck in a sharp breath.

I know Barry, and he's a fucking perv. The number of times he's bragged about banging a client during a tattoo appointment makes me sick. "Did he touch you inappropriately?" *Look at me, asking such questions when I've had my hands all over her and my tongue in her mouth.* Her face drops, and she shrugs. I grip her chin and bring her eyes back to mine. "Did. He. Touch. You?"

She traps her bottom lip behind her teeth, and I peel it free, my patience wearing thin. "Sorta."

Fuck.

I snatch my hands from her and step away, almost knocking over my chair. Pushing my hands through my hair, I study the polished concrete at my feet. Anger causes my chest to heave, and if Barry were in front of me right now, I would lay his ass flat at Soph's feet like a damn sacrifice. She drops from my desk and steps in front of me. Her small hand reaches out, and I'm reminded that I'm not alone and it's not okay to lose my shit.

What is it with assholes taking what's not theirs to take?

"I promise I'm okay. I stopped him immediately and made it clear I wasn't interested … and in case you're worried, you're not doing the same." I fucking know I'm not like Barry. She takes my hands and tentatively places them beneath her breasts. I look down at her, noticing the heat in her eyes and the quiet demand that I touch her. "Please keep touching me."

Her words undo me, and I span my hands across her ribs beneath her breasts, then drop my mouth to hers. She presses up on her toes, sliding her hands around my neck and into my hair. Our kiss escalates quickly, and before I can think twice about it, I pick her up and carry her back to my desk, laying her flat. Her back arches against the cold, and she looks fucking spectacular. I drop my hands to the button on her jeans and check in with her. "Okay if I take these off?"

"Please." I make quick work of the zipper, remove her shoes and socks, and slip the denim from her shapely legs, exposing more tattoos. This time, a delicate lace band around the top of her left thigh and more Henna-inspired work across her lower stomach and pelvis, sinking beneath the top of her matching panties. I try to push away the image of Barry working so close to her pussy, but it's impossible to erase the image. Almost as if she can read my mind, she allays my distress. "Barry didn't do those. After what happened the first time, I got Camryn to do the rest."

My heart settles, and I bury my nose against her pussy, nudging her clit. Drawing a deep breath into my lungs, I murmur against her mound, "You smell perfect. Tell me I can taste you, Soph." I trace my eyes up the length of her body until I capture her gaze as I dip my fingers in each side of her panties. God, she's so beautiful. So perfect.

"If you don't, I might die."

I raise an eyebrow and smirk at her. "We can't have that." She raises her hips, and I make quick work of removing the final garment of clothing, leaving her completely exposed and at my mercy. I push her legs open and study her perfect pussy. Her outer lips glisten with arousal, and I use my fingers to separate them for my perusal. "So fucking pretty." My breaths quicken, and my cock begs for release at the vision before me. "You're so fucking perfect." I blow a hot breath across her pussy lips, eliciting a moan.

"Lincoln?"

"Give me a moment, will you?"

She pushes up, resting on her elbows, and studies me intently. I work to temper my desperation to devour her—every single inch.

I want to mark her.

I want to make her mine.

I want to fuck her so hard she feels me inside of her for a week.

Finally, I dip my head and flatten my tongue against her, licking from her opening to her clit, where I change the shape and pulse the tip against her bud. A soft moan fills the office, and when I glance up, she has her head dropped back and her hands cupping her beautiful breasts. Fuck, that's hot.

"Be a good girl and keep playing with your tits for me while I focus down here." She moans again but does as requested, pressing them together and rolling her nipples like a damn pro. I drop my head and fucking devour her.

I lick, bite, and suck her like a starved man, holding her open with my big hands. She writhes beneath me, pulling her hips away as she arches her back, making a beautiful shape on my desk. I'm not going to be able to work here without this image assaulting me, and if she lets me, I'd love to fucking draw her like this and have it tattooed on my body.

Her moans and sighs increase, and I take that as my cue that she's getting close, so I push a single finger into her tight entrance.

Jesus, she's so fucking small.

Her silken walls are so damn snug around my finger, and my cock grows harder at the idea of being buried in her tight heat. Her fingers glide into my hair, gripping the strands as she presses me into her pussy. Her hips fly up with a long, low moan when I suck her clit hard. "Lincoln." She shakes her head back and forth. "I'm so close. Make me come."

"What do you say?" She opens her beautiful big brown eyes, and adorable creases form between her brows. I raise mine and wait as I slowly glide my finger torturously in and out of her, replacing one with two to stretch her; if I don't, I'll hurt her later.

"Lincoln, don't be cruel."

"Where are your manners, Soph?"

"Please?"

"Please, what?"

She rolls her eyes, but the tilt of her lips suggests she's not upset. "Please make me come."

"Good girl." Extra wetness coats my fingers as I slam inside her heat. She mewls as she arches her back beautifully, preening under my praise. I suck her clit into my mouth in deep pulls as I push my fingers roughly in and out of her opening. "You're so fucking tight. You're gonna strangle my cock, and I'm going to love every second of it."

Her silken walls pulse around my fingers, and she cries out as her legs tighten around my head. Slowing my movements, I keep my eyes on her as she reaches her peak; her mouth dropped open with a silent scream. *She's so damn beautiful.* The sight of her falling apart will be permanently emblazoned on my brain—an extraordinary moment I'll always cherish.

Her body falls lax, and I gently remove my fingers, missing her heat immediately. Softly pressing a kiss to her mound, I push my fingers into her mouth. "Taste yourself." My eyes roll to the back of my head at the way her unfocused gaze watches me while she sucks my fingers clean with a swirl of her hot tongue.

Once my fingers are clean, I slowly rub my hands up her thighs, loosening the tight muscles, then place kisses across the tattoo on her pelvis and abdomen, working my way up to her breasts, which I tease with my tongue before moving up to her mouth.

Her fingers tangle in my hair as she holds me in place, kissing me hungrily and moaning into my mouth. *Could she be any more perfect?*

All at once, her hands leave my hair and slide beneath my shirt, slipping the fabric up my torso to bare my abs. "Take off your shirt, Linc. I need to see you." My muscles twitch while my dick punches against my zipper, and as I drag the offending garment over my head, her hands drop to the button on my jeans. She quickly unfastens it, and I toss my T-shirt onto the chair. Next, her slim fingers are ripping my zipper down and pushing my jeans below my ass. "Hey, what's the rush?"

She pants as she steals her eyes away from my cock, barely tucked away in my boxer briefs, to look up at me. "I need you inside me, Linc." She licks her swollen lips, making them shiny.

I rub my thumb across the bottom pillow. "I like your lips like this."

Her posture softens, and a shy smile touches her bare lips. I lean down and press mine to hers, and for a moment, her hands stall in their mission as I deepen the kiss. I could kiss this woman every day and never tire of her taste. *What the fuck is happening to me?*

Her hands move to my biceps, and she grips them loosely, sliding her hands over the muscles as she peels her mouth from mine and traces her eyes over my exposed upper body. "Mmm, I love your tattoos," she murmurs against my lips.

I don't want to talk about my tattoos right now; we've had enough sadness and I'm aching to be inside her, so I press my mouth to hers again.

Her hand slips beneath the cotton of my briefs to grip my erection, and I groan at the feel of her small hand wrapped around me. She's not shy about it either, which is fucking awesome. A woman who goes after what she wants is such a damn turn-on, so I help her by pushing my briefs down my legs to join my jeans.

Her eyes widen when they land on my cock as it stands proudly against my stomach. "Oh, shit," she breathes.

I slide my hand between her legs and stroke her still-soaked pussy. "Don't worry, Shortcake, we'll take it slow."

Leaning down, I take her mouth in a wicked kiss. It's hot and sexy, and the longer it goes on, the wetter she gets; *so damn responsive.* Her hand continues to stroke me, occasionally swiping her thumb across my slit, making me shiver and testing my patience. I grab her ass and lift her, encouraging her to wrap her legs around my waist so I can grind against her, ensuring her clit gets maximum stimulation.

Her arms wrap around my shoulders, and she rocks, her breasts pressed tight against me, her peaked nipples rubbing the hair on my chest. Her heart beating wildly against mine and her heated skin against mine is better than I could have ever imagined. She's so soft and smooth beneath my touch. Her womanly curves fill my hands like she was born to be mine. Her hot pussy rubs against my cock, making it grow harder and thicker with every stroke, and I'm on the brink of embarrassing myself.

She uses her thighs on my hips to push up and reaches between us to notch the head of my cock at her opening. She's so hot … and wet … and my eager dick weeps to get inside her, but she's small … and she was so tight around my fingers. Pushing down, she takes the head of my cock inside her heat, and I close my eyes, dropping my head back on my shoulders to center myself as a groan rumbles from deep within.

I desperately *want* to shove inside her until I'm buried deep, but I won't.

I don't want to hurt her.

"Linc?" she murmurs against my throat.

"Give me a minute, Shortcake. You feel better than anyone ever has, and I need … I need a minute," I breathe as I look into her bedroom eyes with lust and desperation shining back at me, mirroring my desire.

Why does she feel so different?

I can't put my finger on it, but it's more than the connection I'm experiencing—it's inexplicably deeper, and yet it's not enough.

It will never be enough.

She tries to push down, to take me deeper, to hurry me along, but I grip her ass tightly and frown at her. Licking my throat, she nips my collarbone—*maybe she's not as innocent as I first thought*—and I almost break from her seduction. She slips down a little further, and I groan at the sensation.

Her heat.

The silken feel of her walls as they sheath my cock.

Fuck.

"Your pussy's stretching perfectly to take my cock but you're so tight … I don't want to hurt you," I pant, doing my best to keep myself in check.

Biting her bottom lip, her eyes roll back in her head. "God," she murmurs.

"That's why I want to take it slow." I kiss my way up her throat and slide my hands from her ass along her thighs to open her further, then push in a little more.

"Mmm," she hums, but I notice a tightness around her eyes that wasn't there before. She readjusts her position slightly, opening her a little more to my slow intrusion.

Leaning down, I take her mouth in a heated kiss meant to distract her. I caress my tongue along hers, twisting and tasting, stroking and sucking. She slips down my dick a little further, and I hold her still so I can relish the feeling of her velvet walls wrapped around me. This woman is going to undo me and at thirty-eight, it's been a long time since that happened.

She winces.

"You okay?"

"It's been a long time, and it's a tight fit, but I will be."

My chest puffs up. A *long* time. "How long?" The words escape my mouth before I can stop them.

Her bottom lip slides behind her teeth and her eyes slip to the side. "Uh."

Shit, that was probably too personal. But, hey, I have my dick mostly inside her. That's pretty personal, and I really want to know, but maybe it was inappropriate. "That's ok—"

"Close to nine years."

"What the fuck?" I hiss as I pull her off my dick, missing her tight heat immediately, and sit her on my desk. When I look down at my angry cock, I realize exactly why she felt so amazing—I forgot the condom.

Let's not mention she's almost a virgin, for fuck's sake.

Can a woman be revirginized? Is that even a thing? I grab

her panties and slip her feet roughly through the openings like I'm dressing a child.

She frowns at me and pushes at my hands. "What are you doing?"

"I thought it was obvious. I'm dressing you."

"I know that. I want to know why you stopped?" Her arched brows dip low over her eyes, but I continue to drag her panties up her legs. *She's not helping at all.*

I tap her hip. "Lift."

"No. Not until you tell me why you stopped and suddenly you're dressing me like I'm a damn child." She slaps my hands away.

I release her panties and push my hands through my hair, then drop my eyes to the floor, noting my now almost-flaccid dick. I wave my hand in the proximity of my pelvis. "I don't have a condom. I never fucking forget to suit up."

Her eyes widen, and she finally lifts her ass to pull her panties into place. Thank fuck she finally covered her pussy. Now I don't feel quite so filthy.

Nine years. Nine fucking years since she's had sex. That would have made her—I quickly do the calculations in my head—seventeen!

Shit!

No wonder she's so fucking tight.

—sophie—

My cheeks flame with embarrassment. He can say he stopped because he realized he wasn't wearing a condom, but it seems suspiciously coincidental he came to that realization when I told him how long it had been since I'd had sex.

Well … to be fair, sex *with* someone else. I have sex *all* the time. *On my own.* With the help of my books, a secret stash of toys, and my amazing shower head.

I hop from the desk and gather my jeans, pulling them roughly up my legs. My bra's next, followed by my silk blouse. With each article of clothing I put on, I strengthen my armor to shield my humiliation. I can't believe I offered myself to him on a platter, and he's rejected me.

He seemed so into it; so into me.

"Soph—"

I hold up my hand. "Please don't say anything. I'm embarrassed. Mortified actually. I just want to dress, go home, and wash this all away."

I can't look at him as I shove my feet into my Chucks without socks. As I push past him to escape the office, he grips my arm. "I'm sorry. You have nothing to be embarrassed or mortified about. This was entirely my fault. I went too far. This never should have happened between us." He roughly pushes his hand through his messy hair. "I'm twelve fucking years older than you, *and* I'm your boss. You deserve better than a fuck in the back office, Sophie, and you shouldn't settle for anything less after nine years of abstinence." He forces my chin up with his fingers until he has my eyes. I try to slide my gaze away, but he follows me and fills my vision. "You deserve more than being fucked by an old guy like me." He tenses his jaw. "You should be with a guy closer to your age."

"Yeah, well, pretty sure I'm old enough to decide where, by who, and how I want to be fucked. Good night. See you tomorrow, *boss*," I snap and push past him on shaky legs, humiliation and anger flooding my system. Things were going so well. If only I'd kept my mouth shut. I'd be screaming out a perfect orgasm right about now.

There's no way I can come back tomorrow.

My alarm blares, and I wake with a groan. My eyelids feel glued shut from my tears last night. Covering my face with my hands, I relive my mortification. There's absolutely no way in hell I can go to work today.

I can't face him.

Not today.

Maybe tomorrow.

Even that may be a stretch.

What was I thinking?

Oh, right. I wasn't. Just as I didn't think nine years ago with Paul when I happily gave him my virginity in the backseat of his car after prom—and we all know how that worked out for me. Not that I'd ever change history. If I did, I wouldn't have James, and he's the best thing I've ever done.

I throw the covers back and move through my morning routine so I can get James ready for school. The great thing about starting work at nine forty-five is that I can take James to school every day, and he only has to catch the bus home. Dad wheels himself to the bus stop down the road to collect him, and they enjoy the afternoon snack I prepare for them before I leave for work. Dad cooks dinner on the nights I work, and I cook on the nights I don't, which means I can give him an extra break tonight because I'm not going into work today.

James is zipping up his jeans when I walk into his bedroom. His eyes light with happiness when they land on me. "Mom!" He dives for me.

I chuckle as he flings his arms around me. He's already up to my shoulders, and I don't think I have too much longer to enjoy his boyish ways before he'll be too cool to greet me with this much enthusiasm, so I hug him close, drawing his scent into my lungs. "Did you miss me?"

He pulls away and nods wildly. "Grandad and I missed you heaps, but we had a boys' night, which was pretty cool."

"A boys' night, huh?" I ruffle his hair.

"Yeah. We had root beer and pretzels and watched a game of soccer. Grandad yelled at the TV when the referee made a bad call. He was so funny." A pang hits my chest that James doesn't have his father around; someone who could take him to games or play with him in the backyard. "I really liked watching soccer. My friend, Josh, plays. Do you think I could play?" he asks with a hopeful grin.

"Uh, that might be tough with me working until dinner-time. Can you ask Josh more about it, and we'll see if it works with my schedule? I can also ask Hope where Evan plays soccer. His practice may work with my schedule if Josh's doesn't."

"Yes!" He throws his fist into the air. "Thanks, Mom."

If I can make it work, I will. I'd love for him to play sports, but I don't want to ask Dad to take him. I try to do most of the parenting, and Dad's great about not stepping in unless I ask for help, which I try not to do more than I already have. He lets us live with him, for goodness' sake—he already helps us plenty. I brush my son's hair out of his eyes, then tell him to meet me in the kitchen for breakfast.

James tells me about his day yesterday while I make breakfast, lunch, and afternoon snacks. Dad's still sleeping, which is common when he works on his manuscript until late, so I try to keep our noise to a minimum.

I drop James at school and tell him I'll pick him up so he doesn't have to catch the bus. You would think I told him I'd bought tickets to Disneyland with how excited he was. I figure I can take him out after school, since I'm home today. Stopping at the store, I grab what I need for fish quesadillas and head home.

"Is that you, Sophie?" Dad calls from the back of the house as I step inside, a note of worry in his tone.

"Yeah, it's me," I call.

His toast is frozen halfway to his mouth, and the furrows across his forehead are deep when I step into the kitchen. "Why are you home?"

I shrug. "I don't feel one hundred percent."

He pushes away from the table. "You're not coming down with something, or did you drink too much last night when you were out with your friends?" The disapproval in his voice is thick as he asks. He's very anti-alcohol since the truck driver that caused the derailment was intoxicated.

"No, Dad. I didn't drink last night." I turn my back to him to put the fish in the fridge and hide my lie. Technically, it's not a lie. I *didn't* drink last night. "I think something I ate has disagreed with me. I'm gonna take it easy today."

"Do you need to report the restaurant for food poisoning? That's most unsatisfactory, Soph."

I chuckle. "I don't think so, Dad. I don't think I have food poisoning … just an upset stomach. I'll be fine with a little rest. But I'll cook dinner tonight, okay?"

He nods. "Okay. Did you let your boss know you're unwell?"

I guess I should send Linc a message. "Not yet. I'll do that now." I finish putting the groceries away, kiss Dad on the cheek, and retreat to my bedroom.

Dragging out my phone, I chew on my bottom lip when the time stares back at me. I should be arriving at work right now. I wonder if Lincoln has a cup of coffee waiting for me at the reception desk. I know they'll manage just fine without me, but it will be inconvenient when they need to stop to answer the phone and greet clients.

I pull up Lincoln's number and type a message.

ME

I'm sorry, I won't be at work today

I need to take a personal day

I delete the message. Damn. Is he going to be pissed? Or is he expecting me not to show up today? Or maybe he'll fire me. My stomach sinks at the thought of our carelessness costing me my job.

Maybe I'll send a message to Ken instead. Cowardly, I know.

ME

Hey Ken

Can you please let Lincoln know I won't be in today?

> I don't feel well and I don't want to get you
> guys sick

I jump when my phone buzzes straight away.

KEN

> Sorry to hear you're sick, doll

> Why don't you message Linc yourself?

ME

> I don't want to bother him

I watch the screen with a galloping heart, but nothing comes through. I don't know whether to be thankful or worried. I know I'm going to have to pull up my big girl panties tomorrow, but today, I want to block out the world and hide from my embarrassment.

Dad's writing in his office, James is in bed, and I'm sketching on the couch when a soft knock sounds at the front door. I glance at the time. Ten. It's late for someone to be at the door. Maybe if I ignore it, they'll go away.

I focus back on my sketch. Even though I didn't go to work today, I've spent the day adding to my portfolio. Lincoln wants to photograph some of my sketches and post them on the studio's Instagram page to gauge interest. He thinks I'll be ready to tattoo my first person next month at the rate I'm progressing on the fake skin. I feel giddy thinking about the day I tattoo my first real person.

A louder knock jolts me. Damn. I drop my sketchpad and climb to my feet, then pad to the front door. Looking through the side glass panel, I almost fall on my ass when I see Lincoln standing on my porch, his back to the door.

Shit!

What should I do? Do I ignore him and pretend nobody's home, or do I face the music?

He knocks again, and I glance over my shoulder.

I don't want Dad coming to investigate and I guess it's better to get this over and done with now, instead of at work tomorrow in front of Ken. Pushing my shoulders back, I suck in a deep breath, finding my fortitude. I swing the door open and quickly step outside, quietly closing it behind me. I definitely don't want Dad to overhear this conversation.

Lincoln spins around, his eyes scanning me from head to toe like he can see what's going on inside my body, and I realize I look very different from how I dress for work without my teased hair, makeup, and dark clothes. Instead, charcoal leggings hug my hips, and a soft pink sweater falls off one shoulder.

"What are you doing here?" I ask quietly, folding my arms across my body.

He pushes his hand violently through his hair, and his shoulders drop as he releases a harsh breath. "Soph." My name shatters across his lips almost painfully. "I-I was worried about you. About what happened. I don't want you to leave. I know how important this job is to you. It's something you were born to do, and I don't want to jeopardize that because I couldn't keep my hands or dick to myself."

Air leaves my lungs in a whoosh, and the stiffness in my muscles dissipates at his pained expression and the sorrow in his voice. "Lincoln," I murmur.

"No. Let me finish. I'm incredibly sorry, Sophie. I have no excuse. No explanation for my behavior." He holds out his hands, palms up. "I've never done anything like that before, and I don't expect you to believe me, but it's God's honest truth. I've been pissed at myself all day, and I don't blame you for staying away, but I hope you'll come back. You're too talented to give up your dream, and I don't want to be the asshole who gets in your way." He steps closer like he can't bear the distance between us and tilts my chin up. "Sophie," he says my name with a deep rumble that vibrates through my body and makes a direct hit at my core. "I need to apologize for putting my hands on you. It was inappropriate, and I don't want you to think I do that sort of thing with my employees. It's never happened before, and I assure you it won't happen again. You're safe working with me." *Well, that's a little disappointing.* "I'm not some handsy asshole who takes advantage of women." *I wouldn't mind being taken advantage of by him. Sigh.*

I nod the best I can with his knuckle supporting my chin. "I know that." And I do. I've never once felt a creepy vibe from him. He scans my face and nods sharply. I expected him to be angry; I never anticipated this, and I'm unsure how to deal with it. I blink quickly and swallow to hold back the sting of tears threatening to escape. "I was always coming back tomorrow. I just needed today to get over my embarrassment," I whisper into the night.

He moves closer still, like he's as drawn to me as I am to him, and his familiar cologne wafts around me, easing my anxiety over the situation. "You have nothing to be embarrassed about. It's me who should be embarrassed. I'm old enough to know better, and I shouldn't have taken advantage of you in a vulnerable moment. It was so far beyond wrong."

He doesn't deserve to carry all the burden. I rest my hand over his tattooed forearm, growing more settled now that part of me is touching part of him. "It wasn't entirely your fault. I was wrong, too." I drop my eyes from his. "I'm insanely attracted to you, and I wanted what happened between us to happen." I lick my parched lips. "I've wanted it for a while."

He groans and almost looks defeated as he throws his head

back to look up at the night sky. "You can't say shit like that. I'm trying to do the right thing here, Shortcake."

I shuffle closer until we're almost touching. I don't know where my bravado is coming from, but I grip it with two hands and hold it tight. "The right thing was when you had your head between my legs, and I was crying out your name."

"Fuck! Don't do this to me." He takes a step back and another and another until he's standing on the grass. "Please come back to work tomorrow. I promise to keep my hands to myself and behave in a strictly professional way."

Disappointment is a nasty bitch, but I nod. "I'll be there."

"Good." He jams his hands into his front pockets.

"Goodnight, Lincoln."

"Goodnight, Soph."

CHAPTER 13

—sophie—

I DRAW THE SAME LINE FOR THE SEVENTH TIME. "UGH!" THEN drop my pencil and stare up at the ceiling. The problem is, I have no practical experience with how the lines of this tattoo will look on a bicep—how it'll move or how it'll look as the muscle flexes and contracts.

"What's the problem, doll?" Ken steps into the back office, crunching on an apple, reminding me I should eat my lunch.

I flick my hand out at the sketch I'm working on. "This design. I want it to be perfect, but I don't know how it's going to work with the triceps and biceps as they move."

He nods, taking another bite and chewing as he thinks. "Linc!"

Lincoln pops his head around the doorway. "Yeah?"

"Soph needs your bicep. You got time?"

His eyes narrow as he looks at Ken. "What for?"

Ken looks at me with raised brows as he moves away and leans against the doorjamb but doesn't answer Lincoln, leaving it to me to explain. I tell him my issue, and he moves next to me to study my design concept. I point to the curve that I imagine coming up and wrapping around the inside of the arm. "I'm not sure how far to take this curl or how it will change with movement."

"You could draw it on Linc to give you an idea. He has great biceps." Ken winks and leaves the room.

Flicking my eyes up to Lincoln as my cheeks heat, I stumble over my words. "Uh … you … uh … don't have to do that."

Instead of answering, he sits and rolls closer to me, resting his elbow on the desk and bracketing my thighs with his. "Ken's right. The only way for you to learn it is to draw it." He tips his chin down to his bulging bicep. "Go on. I don't mind." Shifting my eyes between his face and his arm, I tentatively pick up my pen. "I have thirty minutes. Let's go, Soph."

"Thank you," I murmur and my hand shakes as I press my pen to his arm.

"Use your other hand to pull the skin tight. Like you do when you tattoo." His breath ghosts against the side of my face as he speaks.

I glance up at him and swallow my nerves. It's just ink. It'll come off. I tip my head and use my free hand to stretch his skin, then draw the lines on his arm.

His toned, muscular arm.

The one that was holding me up as I shamelessly rubbed my pussy over his dick.

I swallow thickly and try to push the memory away. But I can't. He was so strong, holding me like I weighed nothing. The vision of him keeping me in place as I tried to push down on his dick heats my body and I have to adjust my position to accommodate the ache in my lady parts.

Just focus on the task, Soph.

Pressing my pen against his golden flesh, I draw the first line. It's wobbly at best, so I trace over it to smooth it out, making it more defined. His soft cedar scent surrounds me and settles my nerves and I find myself lost in the design, drawing line after line, curved and straight, thick and thin. Now and then, his muscle twitches, and I glance up to check he's okay—a mistake on my part because I instantly grow self-conscious when I realize his bright blue eyes are locked on me. Clearing my throat, I tuck my messy waves behind my ear. "Thanks for doing this."

"Happy to help." He tips his chin down to my art and our faces are so close that it wouldn't take much for our lips to touch. "You started shaky, but you found your confidence and your lines became clean and strong." He flexes his muscle. "When you use the gun, start with confidence. Tentative strokes won't work."

"Yeah, I realize I need to keep the needle at the same depth."

"You do. It takes practice, but you're well on your way. I've seen a lot of improvement with your practice skins. I think you'll be ready to do some simple tattoos on people sooner rather than later."

My heart bounces around in my chest cavity. "You think so?"

His lips tip up in a devastating smile and those crinkles at the corners of his eyes make an appearance. "I do. Ken agrees. You said you were a fast learner and you've certainly backed up the statement. We're both impressed with your work ethic and eagerness to learn."

My body flushes hot. "Thank you. That … that means a lot to me."

He tips his chin down. "Finish the piece, Soph. I want to see what it looks like."

Dropping my eyes back to his bicep, I press my pen to his flesh and continue with the lines, filling in the design. I make a concerted effort to focus on the work and not on how close I am to Lincoln or how warm and hard his arm feels beneath my touch.

I try to ignore the way his legs bracket mine and how hard his muscular thighs feel when we touch.

I work to block out how his energy vibrates through his body like he's holding himself in check and how my blood buzzes through my veins in answer.

My attraction to him is growing more difficult to suppress, and who could blame me? The man is nothing like I first thought him to be. He's thoughtful and considerate, kind and patient. He's an awesome mentor and a humble artist. Beneath his morning grumpiness, there's a soft side that looks after everyone around him. And hiding beneath his dark T-shirts is a heart of gold. It bothers me how harshly I judged him when he first stormed past me. But worse than that, I hate that I know my father will judge him more harshly and never give him a chance to show his true self.

I finish the design and am happy with how it looks. However, when Lincoln shifts his arm, the lines become distorted, and the design doesn't look how I want. "Ugh, what did I do wrong?"

Lincoln looks down with a smirk. "You didn't position my arm properly. It works better when the client lies down with the arm stretched out, palm up." He lies his arm on the desk and stretches it out flat. "See the difference?"

I study the shape his arm makes this way as opposed to how it looked before. "Right. Gotcha. Why didn't you say anything?"

"The positioning of the body is important for two reasons. The first, as you can see,"—he traces his finger down the length of his bicep while my eyes greedily follow the action—"so the design flows properly with the skin and the muscles, but also so the client is comfortable and can hold the position for a long period. Especially when you're doing sizable pieces." He grins at me with a raised brow. "I didn't say anything because I wanted you to learn this lesson in a way you'd remember."

"Makes sense. Thanks for doing this." I wave at this arm.

"Your design,"—he taps my drawing—"will work perfectly once you consider the best way to position each body part."

"Linc, your client's here," Ken calls from the hallway.

Lincoln turns toward his voice. "Be out in a sec."

I wave at his arm. "Do you want me to clean that off?"

"Nah, I like having your work on me. I may even get you to tattoo something similar when you're ready."

The muscle in my chest makes a sudden departure, landing in my throat. "Really? You'd want my work on your body." His beautiful body.

His eyebrows shoot up. "Why do you sound surprised? You have to know by now I'm a fan of your work." I practically feel like I'm glowing from the inside out because of his praise. He squeezes my shoulder as he stands. "Come on, I'll show you what I mean with my next client while I do a cover-up of an ex-girlfriend's name on the back of his arm."

CHAPTER 14

—lincoln—

I WINCE WHEN I LOOK IN THE MIRROR. I WAS DISTRACTED LAST night and didn't do myself any favors. I still won, but these fucking bruises are going to be a bitch for the next week or so.

Do you want to take a guess at what's been distracting me?

I bet you'll figure it out if you think back to my conversation with my employee on her porch fifteen days ago.

I swear she's been doing everything in her power to tempt me since I told her I'd keep my hands to myself.

It's been fucking torture.

My job used to be my sanctuary; now it's hell.

She's everywhere!

Her seductive curves have even infiltrated my dreams and I wake up with my cock in hand more than I don't, and I swear I can still taste her on my tongue. And let's not talk about the mammoth effort it took to keep myself in check when she was drawing a test tattoo on my bicep. The temptation to kiss her almost won out.

Almost.

"Morning, *boss*," she calls as she breezes through the door.

And that's another thing. She's taken to calling me *boss* in that sexy raspy voice of hers and doesn't that do something to me. I groan under my breath and step out of the bathroom and straight into her lingering coconut scent.

Jesus. Can't a guy catch a break?

"Morning," I grunt, then head to the coffee machine. I make quick work of our coffee, then drop hers at the reception desk.

She looks up at me absently. "Thank you." Her eyes widen when she sees my face and her small hand reaches up. I flinch away and her brows dip. "Tell me the other guy came off worse than you."

I smirk. "The other guy came off worse than me. I was a little distracted, but got my shit under control and laid him flat." All it took was for him to tell me he fucked my little sister last night and he was done, not that he realized the gravity of what he said.

She *tsks* me and steps away. My fighting doesn't impress her like it does most other women, and I find it intriguing. A lot of women find the *bad boy*—or who they perceive to be a bad boy—appealing.

Not that I'm a bad boy.

Yes, I fight.

It started as a way to deal with my anger over my sister being stolen from our front yard, then it turned into a way to make money that I could donate to *Operation Underground Railroad*. They do incredible work supporting victims of child and sex trafficking and do their best to shut down as many operations as they're able.

But she doesn't know that's why I fight.

I stroll to the front door to unlock it, and as I'm heading back toward the office, Sophie grabs my hand and leads me to my station. "Sit." She pushes at my shoulder and I drop into my chair, wincing as I do. She has a tube in her hand as she pushes between my thighs, and I have to close my eyes because her tits are right there.

I could lean forward and suck one into my mouth.

I could make her moan again.

I could do so many things to her.

Things I'm certain she's never experienced. But I *promised*. And above everything, I pride myself on being a man of my word.

When her fingers touch my skin with a gentle press, I open my eyes and study the tube in her hand. "What's that?"

"Arnica. It should help to reduce the bruising." While she tends to the area, her warm eyes remain focused on her task, so I take a moment to study her. She's so beautiful, she hurts my eyes and I wish I were ten years younger. "Do you have bruises anywhere else?"

"Yeah, but I think you'd probably need a bigger tube." I dip my chin toward the tube in her hand.

Her eyes widen. "Take off your shirt."

"Bossy," I huff, but grab my T-shirt at the back of my neck to drag it off. Her gasp is like a gunshot in the quiet room when she sees my ribs.

"Lincoln," she murmurs as her eyes trace the large discolored area across the right side of my torso, following the dark purple contusion as it wraps around my side to my back. She squeezes the tube until a significant amount of the ointment is covering her hand, then she rubs them together and lays them on my ribs. "I'm sorry if this hurts, but hopefully it'll help."

I grunt because having her hands on me has rendered me incapable of speech. She gently massages the ointment over the front of my torso, her eyes glistening. A tear falls over her bottom lash and her bottom lip trembles. I can't stop my hands from reaching for the backs of her thighs to anchor her to me in some way. "Soph," I whisper. "Don't cry."

"Why do you do this to yourself?" She glances up at my

eyes and the pain in hers rips my breath from my lungs in a gush. I shrug. "Tell me, so I understand," she murmurs. "I hate that you fight. Tell me there's a good reason you put your body on the line like this."

I blow out a long breath and start from the beginning. "When I was seven, I was playing in the front yard of our home with my younger sister while Mom was taking a nap. Elizabeth was three, one month off turning four." I push past the acid that always rises from my gut when I think about her. Her sweet face and fierce spirit. "She … uh … she fell over and skinned her knees, so I took her over to the porch, calmed her down, and ran inside to get the first aid kit." I pause for a breath and try to slow my heart rate. Even though it happened so long ago, it's still so fucking raw. "When I came back outside, she was gone." Sophie gasps and I chance a look at her face; she's turned the same color as the cream she's rubbing on my body. "I frantically ran up and down the street looking for her, but she was nowhere to be found. I was inside two minutes, tops." Her soulful gaze is swimming with tears and when she blinks, they drop over her lashes and trail down her gorgeous cheeks. I brush them away with my thumbs as I continue. "I woke Mom, and she called the cops. The neighbors searched the neighborhood until the early hours of the morning, but she was gone. She just vanished." I close my eyes and Mom's accusing glare fills my vision, stealing my breath. "I'll never forgive myself for losing my sister."

"Oh, Linc." She cups my cheeks, bringing my eyes to her teary ones. "You weren't to blame. You were only a kid. There should have been an adult supervising. It should never have been your responsibility to care for her." She wraps her body around mine and tugs me into her breasts in comfort. I suck her intoxicating scent into my lungs, wrap my arms around her, and absorb her sympathy—something I've not allowed myself to accept before.

"Yeah." I've heard that before. "Mom was questioned about it and Dad was beyond furious. They argued constantly after her disappearance and he eventually left." I can still hear him shouting at her as she sobbed. Blaming her. *Always* blaming. "But still … *I* was the one that left her alone and vulnerable."

After long, quiet minutes, she pulls away from me, leaving me adrift, and swipes at her cheeks. Her face is blotchy, her eyes are red, and she sniffs before cupping my bristly cheeks again. "I'll repeat … you were just a kid, Linc. It wasn't your fault, and I'll tell you every day until you believe me." *Every day?* I shouldn't read into her words, but I'd be lying if I said I didn't. She adds more ointment to her hands and moves behind me. Her noisy inhalation makes me look at her over my shoulder. Her eyes are drifting all over my back. "You never said that you were in the photo," she says almost accusingly. I shrug and she returns to her task, massaging the ointment into my flesh tenderly. "It's stunning and so beautifully haunting. More so now that I've learned about your loss and how you feel responsible even though you shouldn't," she murmurs reverently. She's quiet for a long time and I sink into the silence. "D-di-did you ever find her?"

I shake my head, unable to answer her over the emotion clawing at my throat.

"I'm so sorry, Lincoln. Nobody should have to experience that." The genuine sadness in her voice guts me.

The worst thing is not knowing where she is.

Not knowing if my sister is being tortured somewhere or if her suffering is over and she's gone from this world.

I've always hoped she was adopted on the black market by a loving family who couldn't have kids of their own. A family who loved her and raised her with care and kindness. Holding onto that hope is the only thing that's gotten me through my darkest days.

Sophie carefully rubs the ointment into my back, sniffing occasionally, and when her hands leave my body, ice replaces the warmth of her touch. I want to keep her hands on me, but I promised not to cross that line again. She holds my T-shirt up and I take it from her.

"Thank you." For taking care of me and for listening to my sad and sorry tale I want to add but don't. She's the first person I've shared that story with in years and I'm unsure what possessed me to open up to her.

—lincoln—

FUCK.

Me.

She looks damn edible.

Sophie struts in wearing a short plaid pleated skirt and knee-high Dr. Martens that leave her gorgeous thighs bare and I'm sure that when she sits, it will ride up and expose the tattoo wrapped around her left thigh. A cropped T-shirt exposing her midriff completes her outfit, and when she reaches up, she'll reveal the bottom of the tattoo I know to be there. I love that I know she has those tattoos—it's both intimate and torturous.

I drop my head back on my shoulders with a pained groan.

Did I tell you Shortcake's been torturing me non-stop?

She arrives every day looking sexier than the last. She's everywhere I turn with her seductive smile, and I swear she finds any excuse to touch me. I have no idea how I'm supposed to keep resisting her. Especially today.

I'm tattooing one of her designs on a client tonight, which means she's staying late again. And it'll only be the two of us because Ken's leaving early for his grandson's birthday.

I roll away from the table and stretch out my neck. I really must work out a way to remind myself to stretch regularly. Ken's been at me for years about my posture and taking breaks; maybe it's time to listen to the old guy. He wanders around the room to say goodnight to his girls, swapping some pots around so they grow evenly; and my regular client and fight organizer, who's familiar with Ken's attachment to his plants, snickers.

"Man, I'll never get used to a grown-ass man talking to plants the way Ken does," Mike comments.

Ken comes to a stop at my station and points to me. "You need to stretch more often." Then he turns to Mike. "The girls need love, too." He smirks as he spins on his heel and waves over his shoulder. "Good night."

"Night," I call, then roll back to the table to continue my work.

Sophie wanders out from the back after her dinner break and heads straight to Ken's station to clean up. Mike turns his head to follow her. "Your new girl's hot as fuck." His expression turns salacious. "What I wouldn't give to ben—" Anger turns my vision red and I clench my fist, causing the needle to dig into his arm and he curses, "Fuck, man." He looks down at his arm with narrowed eyes and then up at me accusingly. "What the fuck?"

I wince internally, but give him the same look I give my opponent in the ring. If Mike has any sense of self-preservation, he'll pick up what I'm putting down. "Keep your eyes to yourself. She's mine," I snarl.

What the actual fuck?

I had to say something, or I'd hit him. Lay him flat, so he'd stop looking at her like he wanted to … fuck her. *Jesus, is that how I look at her?*

His eyes flick between the two of us, and he points at me. "You"—he points in her direction and I slap his hand down—"pulled that knockout?"

I nod. "Yeah, but she doesn't want anyone to know, so keep it to yourself."

"I'm not surprised. I'd be embarrassed if people knew I was dating you."

"Fuck off," I snap.

He chuckles. "Just kidding. Congrats." When he finally stops laughing, he grows serious as his eyes study my torso like he can see beneath the fabric. "How'd you pull up after last week? You took some heavy hits."

"A bit of bruising, but I'm okay." I grunt and focus back on the feather I'm working on.

Sophie quietly sits to observe, but I ask her to take an inventory of the storeroom. Not that it needs to be done; I just don't want Mike to look at her. When another hour passes and I'm finally finished, relief that he won't be around Sophie any longer washes over me.

"Ah, Linc. That looks amazing. Thank you," he says as he twists his arm back and forth in front of the mirror.

Some of my aches disappear with his awed expression. "You're welcome. Make sure you follow the aftercare."

"Yeah, I will," he answers absently as he studies his new ink.

He heads to reception to pay and I tell Sophie I'm going to take a quick break before our next client arrives. I trust Mike to behave after my warning as she explains the aftercare procedures with him and then prep my station for my last client of the day.

When I step out of the bathroom, Sophie's leaning against

the doorjamb, blocking the entry to the hallway. "You told Mike I'm your girlfriend?"

So much for keeping his mouth shut. I knew I should have finalized his account instead of taking a piss. "He was looking at you and saying inappropriate things about what he wanted to do to you." Her eyebrows shoot up and I lean into her space, lowering my voice. "I was protecting you."

Her casual posture vanishes as her hands fly to her hips and her eyes narrow. "You don't need to protect me. *You* may think I'm too young and incapable of making my own decisions, but I assure you I'm grown enough to take care of myself," she says sharply.

I take a step forward so we're toe-to-toe, towering over her so she has to tilt her head back to keep her narrowed gaze on me. "I know you can take care of yourself, but I will always protect you when men come in here and think they can talk about you in a way that devalues you." I lift my hand to slip a loose lock of silky hair behind her ear. Lowering my voice, I add, "Because I respect you and you're worth more than being treated like a quick fuck." I press a gentle kiss to her forehead and step around her to grab something to eat in the limited time I have.

By the time I step back out to the front of the studio, Sophie has Brielle prepped for me to start work. The full sleeve she's drawn for this Henna-inspired design is spectacular and delicate—*very* Sophie. Ever since I started adding her artwork to our Instagram page, we've had an increase in the number of women contacting us for her designs. This was the first opening we had because of a late cancellation, but there are plenty more on our waitlist. Once her designs make it into the public arena, the requests for her artwork are going to explode. Luckily, she'll be ready to tattoo people within the next few weeks.

I hold out my hand in greeting. "Hey, Brielle. I'm Lincoln. Are you ready?"

She grins at me as her eyes skate down my body. "So ready," she says huskily, like I've just asked her if she's ready for my dick.

I ignore her tone and check over the transfer. "Sophie, you've done an awesome job with this." I glance up at Brielle. "Are you happy with everything?"

She looks down at her arm, scanning the design. "It's gorgeous. Exactly what I wanted."

"Great, let's get started." I take a seat and pick up my gun.

Brielle slides her hand across my arm and rests it over the tattoo representing my sister, making me recoil—I don't like it when clients are so … *familiar*. When I glance at Sophie, she arches her perfect brows. "Please be gentle with me," Brielle says with an air of seduction in her voice, and I have to stop myself from rolling my eyes at her obvious attempt at flirting.

Sophie has a naturally sexy rasp to her voice without trying. Brielle is trying hard to be seductive as she looks up at me with a fake pout and yet she doesn't do a single thing for me. She's a beautiful girl and I would say she's around the same age as Sophie, but she's not my Shortcake.

My Shortcake.

I roll my eyes at myself internally. She's not my anything. Though, the thought of making her mine has crossed my mind more than I'd like to admit.

"I promise you're in expert hands."

She tosses her head back and guffaws, then drops her head and slithers her eyes from the top of my head down my torso, stopping at my crotch. "Oh, I'm sure I am."

For fuck's sake.

She still hasn't removed her hand from me, so I look at it pointedly, hoping she gets the hint. Sophie clears her throat and I flick my eyes up to her face. She presses her lips into a tight line, but the laugh lines around her eyes give her away— she obviously finds Brielle's flirting hilarious.

"Soph, can you please grab Brielle a bottle of water?"

Sophie climbs to her feet with a knowing grin. "Sure thing, hon. Do you want one too?"

"Thanks, Shortcake," I wink at her and she blows me a kiss.

Brielle's eyes widen and she waves her finger between Sophie's vacated spot and me. "You're together?"

I nod. "Yeah." I don't even have to try to sound like a love-struck fool because even though I've done my best to keep the professional lines drawn between us, I like Sophie a hell of a lot more than any employee.

"Oh, I'm so embarrassed. I'll keep my hands to myself. I don't want to step on anyone's toes."

I dip my chin. "I'd appreciate that." Then drop my voice to a whisper. "She can be a little territorial."

Starting the gun, the familiar buzz fills the silence, and I get lost in tracing Sophie's delicate line work. The woman is crazy talented and I'm rapt I convinced Ken to give her a chance. As much as he liked her and loved her work, he was reluctant to bring her on because we're so far behind with our bookings, but she'll soon be up to speed and be able to work on small, straightforward pieces.

Wiping away the last of the excess ink, I peer up at Sophie to check on her emotional state. She's doing well to maintain her professional demeanor; however, I recognize the shimmer in her eyes and the tightness around her jaw as she holds in her emotions. I really hope she's not going to cry every single time someone gets one of her pieces tattooed because I'm never sure how to deal with female tears.

"Done." I roll away from the table and stretch out, groaning like an old man. Once again, I completely forgot to take breaks and stretch.

Sophie climbs to her feet and grabs the mirror so Brielle can see her new art. Her hand flies up to her mouth and her wide eyes take in every detail. "Oh my gosh, it's gorgeous." She flits her eyes between me and Soph. "You guys make a great team. You're both so talented."

I wave my arm out toward Sophie. "All her."

Pink darkens Sophie's cheeks. "Not really. If you didn't work your magic, there wouldn't be a tattoo." I can tell she truly believes that, so I let it go … for now.

I say goodbye and head out back, leaving Sophie to explain the aftercare to Brielle. After a few minutes, Sophie steps into the office as I'm rolling my neck and moves behind me. "You should consider setting a timer or something to remind you to stretch." Her hands land on my shoulders and she rubs her thumbs deep into the base of my skull. She chuckles behind me when I drop my head forward with a groan. *Holy shit, that feels good.*

Her thumbs disappear and I hear a whisper of fabric moving and then her elbows dig into the top of my shoulders. "Fuck," I grunt.

She reduces the pressure with a snicker. "Sorry."

She doesn't sound fucking sorry.

"Nah, that's okay. Keep going. I was just surprised." She digs in deep and I know when she stops, my muscles will feel so much better from the attention she's giving them. "How did you feel about the tattoo tonight?"

Her elbows disappear and her body brushes mine as she moves around to the front of me, pushing me away from my desk and nudging her way between my thighs. My hands automatically move to her hips as hers lift to my shoulders again. She gives me a shaky smile. "I was proud I didn't cry. I was so close, but I held it in." She presses into the front of my shoulders with her thumbs, her eyes watching the movement, but I sense she's trying to avoid eye contact with me. "Will I ever get used to seeing my art on someone's skin?" she whispers.

I shrug. "I hope not. I still feel overwhelmed every time

someone walks out of here with my art on their body. It's fucking awesome that they'll be carrying a little of me everywhere they go. I cherish it and I don't see a problem with the way you feel." I squeeze her soft hips in reassurance. "I think if we stop feeling that way, it means we don't care like we should."

Her lips part on a sigh—she's so damn responsive. "Thanks, Linc."

We fall into a comfortable silence and I drop my gaze from her face, down her sexy throat, and notice her pulse fluttering quickly. Flicking my eyes up to her face, her lips are parted slightly, and I know I shouldn't, but I move forward slowly without overthinking it.

I've tried.

But nobody could fault me for what I'm about to do when she's standing so close. Her coconut scent wafting around us, her hands on my body, and her obvious response to how close we are is making my brain misfire.

I wait for her to react; to pull away, but she doesn't. Instead, she watches with pupils blown wide, filled with lust as I close the distance. A hint of wariness creeps in the closer our mouths get, and I don't blame her after the last time. There's no denying I was a dick.

But this time … I'm not stopping.

"What's changed?" she murmurs against my lips as I make the softest contact.

"Everything."

Nothing.

I'm just tired of fighting.

And even though I renewed my promise to myself a few short hours ago, I won't … *can't* stop this time.

I press harder against her lips and her hands slide up the side of my neck into my hair. She holds me close, as if afraid I'll come to my senses and push her away again. I don't think

I'll survive if I stop this time. And I know she deserves better than this. Than me. But I can't deny myself any longer.

I need her body surrounding mine.

I need to be wrapped in her tight heat.

I need her breath in my lungs and her essence on my tongue.

I need *her*.

Deepening the kiss, I demand entrance with my tongue and she doesn't deny me.

She should.

But I'm going to take everything she's willing to give me this time.

I'm not stopping.

I delve into her mouth and take my time to lick and stroke her, reacquainting myself with her taste, her sighs, her delicate moans. My blood rushes through my veins like a tsunami, straight to my dick, and my body heats to an almost unbearable level.

I need to get us naked.

Sliding my hands from her hips to the dip of her waist, I rub my thumbs along her ribs beneath her breasts, ensuring my nails scrape the fabric of her bra. Her flesh quivers beneath my touch and goosebumps cascade across her body. Her response boosts my need as she pushes into my touch. Moving higher, I slip my hands over her breasts, cupping them reverently as I circle each peak with my thumbs while her heart thunders beneath my touch.

I pull back just enough to ask, "Can I take this off?"

She nods, while I grip the hem of her top so I can remove it. Sliding it from her body, I drop it on my desk behind her, sending her luscious hair cascading down her back. The feminine color of her bra is quite the contrast to the dark skirt, knee-high Dr. Martens, and black top but I sense this woman is full of contrasts if I take the time to get to know her properly—something I want to do with an urge I've not felt before.

I unclasp her bra with one hand and make quick work of removing it, releasing her gorgeous tits straight into my waiting mouth. I suck as much of her flesh as I can and flick her nipple with my tongue while I roll the other one between my fingers. Her body shivers and she moans, raking her short nails through my hair and sending fire licking through my veins.

Her hands scrabble for my T-shirt and she clumsily drags it up my body. Reluctantly, I tear my mouth away and grab the back of the collar to remove it, then squeeze her tits together and bury my face between them, rubbing my stubble-covered jaw across her soft, plump flesh. Her hands grip my hair as she moans. "That feels so good."

I agree.

It feels *so* good that if I don't slow down, this is going to be over before we start and I don't want that. The last time she had sex before me would have been when she was a teen, for fuck's sake. I'm assuming the guy she was with was a kid, too. I want to show her the difference between being with a kid and a man, which won't happen if I lose it too soon.

I pepper feather-light kisses on her lips and pull away, so I can see her face properly. Her lids peel open slowly, revealing her lust-drunk gaze. Slipping my fingers through her silky hair, I secure it behind her ear, watching how her breath catches when I brush the sensitive spot there and the way her pulse flutters as I trace the column of her throat with the back of my hand. Her lips are puffy from our kisses and her eyes study me as intently as I'm studying her. She's so damn beautiful. It's a miracle I've kept my hands to myself this long.

"What do you want me to do to you, Shortcake?" I whisper.

I watch as she swallows. "Everything," she murmurs confidently.

—*sophie*—

So this is happening.

Finally.

I have no clue what's changed for him, but I'm not about to question the turnabout. He kisses me like he's as desperate for me as I am for him and finally, someone wants me as much as I want them. If he stops this time, I don't think I'll ever forgive him and I'll definitely have to find another job, but I don't care.

I *want* this.

I've wanted it for weeks.

His warm mouth closes around my peaked nipple while his fingers tweak and pinch the other. It feels incredible. Pushing further into him, I slide my fingers into his messy hair to anchor myself. When my legs shake with lust, I climb onto his lap for support, tossing my head back when his sharp bite sends electricity shooting through my muscles.

Thick fingers caress my left thigh, and he rudely pulls his mouth away from my boob. "These thighs of yours have been torturing me all day, Shortcake." His fingers move higher, tracing my tattoo, then glide across to the front panel of my panties. "Every glimpse of your tattoo was pure torture." He rubs my pussy with the back of his hand, making me squirm. "I felt like a teenager, waiting for you to bend over or sit, so I could steal another glance." My eyebrows shoot up because he did a damn good job of hiding all of this from me.

He flicks up my pleated miniskirt, exposing my panties to him, then grips my waist and positions me on the edge of his desk, rolling himself closer. He uses his big hands to push open my thighs and his heated gaze drops to my panties, which I'm certain are soaked. If I weren't so turned on right now and desperate for his touch, I would be embarrassed, but the lust filling the space between us suggests he enjoys how wet I am.

His eyes flick up to mine. "Is that all for me?"

Mmm, his voice has grown deeper, more gravelly.

I bite my bottom lip, suddenly shy. Dragging the backs of his knuckles over the wet patch, he licks his lips, then dips his head and presses his nose into the fabric, rubbing my clit with infuriatingly feather-light circles that tease me and drive me crazy at the same time. Leaning back on my hands, I tilt up my hips, but he pulls away and pushes my butt flush with the desk.

"Lincoln," I moan in frustration, digging my fingers into his hair to pull him back to me.

A dark chuckle gusts past his lips. "You in a hurry, Shortcake?"

Guilt that I *should* be in a hurry to get home to James slides down my spine, but I push it away. He'll be asleep by now, so there's no need to hurry Lincoln along. I shake my head. "No. I just want you to make me feel good."

"Oh, I plan to make you feel fucking amazing." His lips tip up in a lazy smirk and he winks at me before tucking his fingers into each side of my panties. "Lift." I follow his command, and he slides the cotton down my legs, scraping his nails along my flesh, and over my boots until they're free. "These hot as fuck boots are staying on and so is that skirt. I've had images of bending you over my desk all day."

My pussy throbs at the image he paints, and I'm certain I'll leave a wet patch on his desk. "God, I want that so much." He drives me crazy with his words.

Lincoln lowers his head with a wicked grin and then his lips touch my knee in a tender kiss. He makes his way up my thigh, kissing my leg until his mouth is in line with my private space. His hand grazes my other thigh, and he uses his fingers to separate my lips. A groan rumbles from deep within and with his eyes locked on the prize, he moves in, pressing my thighs further apart with his broad shoulders.

The first swipe of his tongue sends my head spinning, and the second has my eyes rolling to the back of my head.

Delicate passes over my soft, swollen lips.

He licks my heated flesh, sending my blood racing through my veins to the point it's all I can hear. My heart pounds a heady rhythm that threatens to escape my ribs. When he moves his fingers so he can hold me open with one hand, then slips a long digit inside me, my hips buck. His hot tongue works over my clit in increasingly tight circles and I feel his lips tip into a smile against me when I grip his hair, holding him to me because I might die if he stops.

"I love your hands on me, but can you loosen your grip a little?" he says, with his lips pressed against my pussy.

Oh shit!

I release his hair and massage the area I was abusing as he switches out one finger for two and slams into me roughly, stealing the apology from my lips. I cry out as I push into his hand. "That feels so good."

"You are so fucking hot and tight around my fingers. My dick is gonna tear this little pussy apart." He pushes in deeper and the sound of my wetness fills the office. "I'm going to erase any previous lovers from your memory."

His words send flashes of light zapping through my body, lighting me up to the point I fear my orgasm is going to rip me apart. Every muscle draws tight and my legs close around Lincoln's head as he flicks his tongue over my sensitive nub. My body coils like a spring and as he continues to pump his fingers and lick my clit, the tightness in my body becomes almost unbearable. My panting breaths and moans add to the symphony of sounds in the office while my blood sizzles through my veins.

His eyes lock on mine and I hold his heated gaze—unable to tear my eyes away—as my body detonates into oblivion. His answering groan vibrates against me, creating smaller shock-waves through my body; making my legs shake and stomach quiver.

That was embarrassingly fast.

I drop to my back, spent and wrung out, my muscles like liquid. There's no way I can go back to using my toys now. They're sorely lacking compared to Lincoln's mouth and fingers, along with the scruff of his jaw, his powerful body between my legs, his hair tickling my stomach, and his wicked words.

A satisfied sigh bursts from my lips as I drop my hands to my still-quivering stomach, my legs dangling off the end of Lincoln's desk. I don't even have the energy to be embarrassed about my state of undress. His large hands slide up and down my thighs in a soothing caress while he presses soft kisses to my bare mound.

The sound of a drawer opening and closing, followed by rustling, has me lifting my head. He tosses a condom on the desk next to me with a raised brow. "I'm prepared this time." His lips tip up on one side and I push up, ready to rid him of his clothing.

Maybe this isn't as sudden as it seems.

As I sit, he leans in, delving his fingers into my hair and gripping the strands, pulling my head back and locking his gaze with mine. Blue flames study me, skating over my features, cataloging every freckle and blemish. I try to move my head, to kiss him … *anything*, but he holds me in place. "Lincoln?" I murmur. I hope he's not noting how much younger I am than him and he's going to tell me he can't do this for some inane reason.

He brings his fingers up and presses them between my eyes, stroking away the creases caused by my confusion, and his eyes dip to my lips. "You're so fucking beautiful, Soph. All flushed from your orgasm, eyes dazed, skin flushed and glossy." He nudges my nose with his and presses our foreheads together. "Before I destroy you, I want you to know how much I value this gift you're giving me. I want you to know how much I respect you because I'm about to disrespect you in the best possible way." He pulls away and uses my hair to drag me from the desk. "Now drop to your knees and take out my cock." My pussy gushes. *Gushes*. With wide eyes and my heart trying to crack through my ribs, I shakily reach for his button. Resting my hand on the impressive bulge trapped behind his zipper, I pause to soak in the moment. My fingers shake as I unfasten it and drag the zipper down to reveal dark green boxer briefs. I lick my lips at the sight of the darker patch on his boxers and rub my wet thighs together. "Take it out, Soph," he demands, the deep rumble of his voice dripping with lust.

I nod, dragging his underwear down, releasing his heavy cock. It bounces free and I catch it on my tongue. I only hope Lincoln doesn't notice how inexperienced I am. I've never done this before. The idea of sticking Paul's dick in my mouth was gross at seventeen. However, I can't wait to get my mouth on Lincoln. I want to please him, so I wrap my hand around the base of his dick and swallow as much of him as I can. His hips punch forward as a wild groan barrels out of him when his cock hits the back of my throat. Unprepared, I sputter and pull my mouth away so I can catch a breath. "Sorry."

He cups my cheek, his eyes burning with intensity. "Slow

down, Shortcake. I don't expect you to take all of me in that pretty little mouth of yours on the first try. We'll work up to that," he assures me with a wink.

Taking a deep breath, I try to relax, to calm down, to slow my racing heart. Once I'm more composed, I swipe my tongue through his slit and his abs contract deliciously. *So sexy.* I trace up his body with my eyes, along that sexy trail of dark hair from his cock to his navel, over the hills and valleys of his abs, up to his tense pecs, peaked nipples, and those two words inked over his heart, *always remember*. The flush of goosebumps across his tanned and still lightly bruised skin shows he's as affected as I am, settling my nerves.

He's so beautiful.

His fingers dive into my hair and he grips it, holding my head still as he pushes past my lips with a shallow thrust. I grip the base of his cock and stroke it in time with his movements, but he's being too careful and I don't want careful.

I want desperate.

I want wild.

I want *wicked*.

Reaching around him, I grip his ass, relax my throat, and press him into me until I can feel almost every inch of him.

"Fuck, Soph!" he gasps and the woman inside me smirks with satisfaction that I can make someone as experienced as him unbalanced.

Swallowing, I breathe through my nose, looking up at him with tears blurring my vision—brown eyes to the perfect blue flames of his—and I suck, lick, and stroke him. I devour him as he thickens in my mouth, making it almost impossible to continue. He groans, loosening his grip on my hair to stroke it reverently.

Carefully.

Lovingly.

What I see in his stare undoes me.

It's too deep.

Too connected.

And I'm unsure if he means for me to see it, so I break contact and slide him out of my mouth, drawing in a much-needed breath, then take him to the back of my throat again with determination. Squeezing his ass, I drag one hand around to cup his balls to tease them like I've seen women do in some videos I've watched. His abs ripple and tense and panting groans escape his lips, stealing the silence in the office. With each pump of his hips and sexy sound escaping his throat, I grow wetter, and my empty center aches.

Tears escape down my cheeks and excess saliva dribbles out of my mouth, and while I should be more concerned about how I look, the heated stare directed my way puts any worries to rest. His fingers grip my hair, and he drags me off his heavy cock. "You're doing so good, Soph, but I don't want to come down your throat." He releases his grip. "Not this time."

CHAPTER 17

—lincoln—

FUCK ME, SHE'S GOT A MOUTH ON HER.

She comes across as innocent and inexperienced, but she's a seductress in disguise. All sweet curves, delicious valleys, addictive flavors, and moans that are as dangerous as a siren's song.

I scoop her up and fold her over my desk, sliding my hand down the curve of her graceful spine until I reach the fabric at her waist. My glistening cock taps against my stomach as I push the plaid material over the curve of her sexy ass, exposing her to me. Bending at the knees, I swipe my fingers through her slit, causing a groan to shudder from my lips as I collect her arousal. "You're fucking dripping for me. Did you enjoy sucking me off?"

Arching her back, she moans as my wet fingers connect with her swollen clit. "I—" I press the swollen nub, then pinch it. "I loved it. I didn't want to stop."

Continuing my ministrations, I fold over her, cloaking her with my much bigger body. "You're such a filthy girl, you almost made me come before I was ready." I nip her ear and then lick the spot.

She tilts her head to the side with a moan, offering me her neck and I take her invitation to bite the delicate curve where her neck meets her shoulder, then suck it to soothe the sting. She pushes her ass into me and my cock slides between her cheeks, nestling between the plump flesh, dragging me back to the brink.

I desperately need to be inside her.

Grabbing the condom, I quickly roll it down my length, then fist the base to line it up with her slick opening. Intense heat radiates from her pussy as I notch the head of my aching cock, driving me insane. And as her pink lips stretch around my tip, it's impossible to tear my gaze away from the sight of her taking me inside. "Open your legs wider for me, Shortcake."

She does as I ask, arching her spine beautifully as I push inside, achingly slow. Everything inside of me screams to take her hard.

To make her mine.

To *own* her.

But common sense prevails.

It's been a long time for her, and I need to go slow.

There'll be time enough to ruin her.

I push in another inch, giving her a chance to grow accustomed to my thickness. "Your pussy's taking me like the good girl she is," I praise and her walls flutter around me. In this position, she's fucking tight as her silken walls fist me, welcoming me *home.*

Such a simple concept, but something settles deep inside me. Like I've found a missing piece somehow. So fucking cliché. Never thought I'd be *that* guy.

She turns her head to look at me over her shoulder. "Lincoln," she moans, trying to push her hips back. "I need you."

I squeeze her hips roughly and raise my eyes from our joining to meet hers. The heat and desperation I see there almost have me slamming inside like my instincts beg me to do. "I need to go slow. I don't want to hurt you. You're so fucking tight."

"Mmmm." Her eyes roll as I push in a little further, then withdraw, only to push in further still.

I continue the process, torturing us both until I'm seated fully inside. Closing my eyes, I drop my head back on my shoulders, taking a moment to gather myself. I want this to last. I want to make her come again before I do, but with the way she tightly wraps around me, I'll need to draw on every ounce of control I have.

My years of experience. Those twelve years between us need to count for something.

Once I'm confident I won't come in two seconds, I open my eyes and drop my head, taking in Sophie bent over my desk, waiting patiently for me. The way my pelvis is tucked tightly against her backside and the shape of her body. The trust she's giving me blows my mind and fills every cell of my body with gratitude that she walked into my life.

With hot possessiveness to be her last lover.

Fuck!

This pocket-sized woman holds power over me I never would have considered possible. Devotion and loyalty grow in my chest and spread through my body. I want to worship this woman for as long as she'll allow me.

She was made for me just as I was made for her.

I fold my body over hers and take her mouth in a slow kiss. One I hope expresses this means something to me.

That *she* means something to me.

Our teeth clash at this angle, but I don't stop. I'm too raw and I need this connection to ground me. She teases my tongue with hers and I move my hips in a languid dance—slowly retreating and filling her silky heat, matching the action with my tongue in her mouth.

When we pull away to catch our breath, our eyes catch and lock, and I wonder if the vulnerability I see in hers is mirrored in mine. Can she see how affected I am by her? How much I want to keep her?

The need to move. To mate. To fucking snap my hips and bury myself deep burns my muscles.

Kissing my way along her jaw to her ear, I blow a hot breath along her cheek, then rub the scruff on my jaw across the smooth area. "Are you ready, Shortcake?" She nods, her bottom lip trapped between her teeth. "I need your words," I tell her, then kiss her shoulder as I slowly withdraw.

Her eyes widen slightly, and she nods, humming her agreement. Then remembers she needs to speak. "I'm so ready. My body's on fire for you. Please move."

It's all I need. I snap my hips forward so fast that my head spins as her walls spasm around my length. Pushing up from my prone position, I grip her hips and reluctantly drag my cock from her heat. My eyes drop to the slickness coating the condom and a sudden rush of desire to do this bare overwhelms me.

Don't be foolish dickhead.

She wiggles her hips, tempting me to move. I snap my hips forward like I want to drill through her body, shunting my desk forward at the same time with the force. Delicate grunts leave her lips as I rut into her like the fucking animal I am. My desire to be gentle for her first time in so long, forgotten.

Desperation takes its place.

Pure need and desire.

Raw lust and instinct taking over.

My hips snap and withdraw without guidance from me in a dance that's as innate as breathing. Our moans and gasps lance through the air, my hips slap against Sophie's ass, and the desk scratches against the concrete floor, creating a soundtrack that's so damn erotic I can't stand it.

Another slam of my hips. Another moan from Sophie's swollen lips and her walls tighten around my cock, sucking me in deeper. So deep, that I swear I can touch her soul. Her very center. The core of who she is.

My blood fizzes and tingles.

My focus narrows to us.

To the primal place where we're joined and the parts of her I can't see but feel deeply connected to. Our skin glistens with perspiration while red blotches decorate Sophie's tender flesh as her body takes my punishing strokes.

I snap my hips and Sophie's walls pulse. She's getting close, so I tangle my fingers in her hair and tug her head back, holding her in place. "Come on, Shortcake. Don't hold back on me now. Give me everything. Every moan. Every shudder. Break apart and know I'll put all of your pieces back together."

Her pussy spasms around my cock as I rut into her relentlessly, while her spine makes a beautiful shape as it bows when she cries out. With her head tugged back and her body tight and shuddering, she falls apart.

Her pussy sucks me in and holds me tight.

It's fucking magnificent.

Gritting my teeth to hold back my release, I slow my hips, teasing her through her orgasm until she collapses. Her cheek flush against my desk, her hair an absolute mess, and her eyes pressed closed. The muscles in her back move up and down with each inhale and exhale and her lips tip up lazily.

When she slowly opens her eyes, she twists her head and looks at me with a lazy gaze and a satiated smirk. "That was better than any of my toys."

Laughter bubbles from deep within and bursts out of me. "You're so damn unexpected, Soph."

She shrugs off my comment and the need to pull her into my arms becomes too intense. Holding the base of my dick to keep the condom in place, I carefully withdraw, then help

Sophie up from her prone position. Turning her around, I collect her in my embrace and kiss her with all the desire and lust I have for her, but also with a promise that I'll always take care of her.

Her hands slide around my body until she's cupping my shoulder blades as our tongues stroke and tease, lick and taste. We've kissed before, but this feels like we've been doing it for a lifetime already. It feels like we were always meant to kiss each other. Like we were made for each other.

Without tearing my mouth from hers, I slip back inside her welcoming heat, pushing her thighs open wide. She swallows my groan and I pull away slightly to press my forehead to hers. "I need a minute."

Her fingers trace my shoulder blades, then graze down the planes of my back, making my muscles twitch beneath her touch. "Take all the time you need. I love having you inside me. I feel so full … so right," she murmurs against my mouth.

"You feel goddamn incredible around my cock." I press my mouth to hers, swiping my tongue across the swollen pillows, and stealing my way inside. "You were made for me," I murmur against her lips.

Moving my hips in slow, leisurely thrusts, I take my time to build her toward another orgasm. That'll be three. She has a lot of years to make up for and I intend to help her do that. Now that I've experienced the beauty of being inside her, she'll be lucky if I ever leave.

"Linc," Sophie murmurs desperately as her hips move to match mine.

I can't get deep enough like this and I need to bury myself in the center of her being. Gripping her curvy ass, I lift her off my desk. "Wrap your legs around me." She does, locking her feet around my hips. Spinning around, I press her back against the wall and rut into her. My hips piston relentlessly and when I slide my hands around her thighs to open her further, I sink that much deeper into her tight heat. A groan vibrates from my core, rumbling up my throat and past my lips. Sophie swallows it, meeting it with one of her own.

With her arms wrapped around my shoulders, her tits pressed tightly against my chest, she bounces on my cock. "You're so deep like this." She moans into my ear, her hot breath coating the side of my face, sending my need to come into the stratosphere. Her fingers slip up into my hair and tighten around the strands.

Lightning flashes through my veins and my muscles shake with the need to release. I drop my head to suck one of Sophie's nipples into my mouth as I continue to snap my hips, adjusting the angle to hit *the* spot inside her. I need her to fucking come. The telltale sign of her impending orgasm as she fists around me has relief firing through my synapses.

"God, I'm so close again," she exclaims, a tinge of disbelief in her voice. Her short nails claw my shoulders and I tighten my grip on her sensational thighs.

"Give it to me, Soph," I grunt as lightning shoots down my spine toward my balls.

Drawing on every reserve I have, I piston my hips with long, deep strokes. Her tits slide against my pecs with every thrust and the sensations are almost too much. I slam my mouth down on hers and attack her tongue with rough strokes —stealing her breaths as my own. Desperation takes over, and I grab her ass cheeks and squeeze. Her walls clamp tight and the rhythmic tensing of her internal muscles sends me flying over the edge.

A kaleidoscope of color fills my vision as I pull Sophie away from the wall so I can wrap my arms around her and hold her tight. Nuzzling her neck, I groan as I bury myself one last time and fill the condom with my release. Wave after wave of hot cum and for the second time tonight, I wish I wasn't wearing a condom—that my release was filling her. A concept so completely foreign to me, it takes me by surprise.

My body shudders against hers as she wraps her arms around me, holding me as tight as I'm holding her. Our chests expand and deflate rapidly with our breaths, and our hearts pound with a frantic rhythm.

Her hands slip into my hair and her mouth finds mine. I open eagerly, wanting this experience to last as long as possible. Without severing our connection, I find my chair and sit. Our kiss deepens and as we get lost in it, Sophie moves her hips slowly, taking us both over the edge again.

CHAPTER 18

—sophie—

I can't peel my eyes away from Lincoln.

Every twitch of his muscles and every movement of his hand brings forth erotic memories from what we did last night and again this morning. I had to soak in the tub when I got home and I slept the best I have in a long time. I guess several intense orgasms will do that.

My body vibrates with a chuckle as I finish cleaning Ken's station so I can observe Lincoln as he tattoos his client's side with an image of a nineteen-fifties pin-up girl.

The vibration of my phone against my butt startles me, but I ignore it. Even though Linc said I could have my phone with me, I don't want him to think I'm taking liberties now we've slept together. The vibrating stops and immediately starts again. A prickling sensation crawls down my spine, and the need to check my phone becomes overwhelming. The vibrating stops, and I exhale a relieved breath, but it starts again.

Lincoln raises his head. His dark eyebrows slashed low over his gorgeous blue eyes. He gestures with his chin toward my pocket. "Do you need to get that? Someone seems desperate to get in touch with you." The buzzing stops, then starts again.

"Do you mind?" I stand, digging into my back pocket, but don't pull out my phone, waiting for his approval.

"It seems it may be important. Take it in the office."

I nod once—"Thanks."—then take quick steps into the office to check the screen. Four missed calls from Dad. Shit. It vibrates in my hand again, and I immediately accept the call. "Dad, I can't answer the phone whi—"

"I'm so sorry. I fell asleep. I was up late last night writing. I didn't even realize how tired I was until I woke up with my cheek stuck to my keyboard," he blurts in a rush.

"Dad, slow down."

"I can't slow down. I was late to collect James from the bus stop, and he wasn't there!" he shouts, frantic.

My heart drops to my feet, and the world around me slows. The blood in my veins moves like molasses, and my brain pounds. I grip Lincoln's desk to hold myself up before I collapse onto the office floor. "Wha …"

"Did you hear me? James wasn't at the bus stop. He knows the way home from there. It's not that far. He couldn't have gotten lost. He's missing, Sophie! It's all my fault!" He sobs, and I can picture him frantically rubbing his free hand through his thick salt and pepper hair.

My head pounds, filled with cotton and stealing my ability to think. I'm sure there's a logical explanation. There has to be. "Maybe he missed the bus, and he's still at school?"—*that has to be it*—"Or maybe he went to a friend's house? Have you checked with Tyler down the street?"

"Of course I checked with Tyler," he snaps. "He said they got off the bus together. He said James started walking home on his own."

Dizziness overwhelms me, and acid creeps up from my stomach, so I run to the bathroom, banging through the door noisily. I make it just in time for my lunch to reappear, dropping my phone to the floor as I crash to my knees.

"Fuck! Sophie, what happened?" Steady hands gather my hair and pull it out of the way as I empty the contents of my stomach.

"Sophie!" Dad's tinny voice calls from the phone on the tiled floor. "Sophie! Are you okay? What's happening?" His voice is frantic through the speaker, but I'm incapable of speech right now as more of my lunch evacuates my body. I don't recall eating all that much, but this seems never-ending. My hands shake, sweat coats every inch of my skin, and I grip the porcelain tighter so I don't end up face-first in the bowl.

"Hello? Who's this?" Linc's stern voice echoes in the bathroom. *Oh God!*

"Sophie's Dad. Who's this?" Lincoln must have put the call on speaker because Dad doesn't sound so far away. I retch again, and there's nothing delicate about it as bile works its way out of my body.

"Lincoln. Sophie's boss."

"Is she okay? What's going on?"

"She's sick. What did you say to her? She was fine before your call," he snaps, danger and protectiveness in his tone.

"I … uh … told her James is missing." Oh my God! I need to get my shit together. I need to find my son. Strong arms loop beneath mine and help me stand as I try to push up from the toilet. "She needs to come home immediately. I've called the police. They're on the way."

"Sure. Uh, okay. I'll help her clean up, and we'll be on our way."

"Thank you." The relief in Dad's voice is palpable, but I'm unable to find any relief in this situation.

Lincoln helps me to the sink and turns on the faucet so I can rinse out my mouth. My legs tremble, and my body shakes. Tears sting the back of my eyes, and a sob escapes. Tenderly, Lincoln turns me away from the sink and wipes my face with a towel, his concerned eyes following each movement. "There," he whispers. "All clean."

"I-I-I ha-have t-t-to go."

He nods. "Just give me a sec." Before I can answer, he disappears, then returns just as quickly. Cupping my elbow, he leads me toward the back door, grabbing my purse on the way. "C'mon. Let's go." The next thing I know, Lincoln's tearing out of the parking lot and pulling onto the street.

We drive in silence; me looking out of the window, trying to make sense of what's happened. James has to be okay. He *must* be somewhere.

A kid can't just disappear.

Vanish into thin air.

Then I remember what happened to Lincoln's sister.

She vanished into thin air.

I cover my mouth to stem the sob that's forcing its way up my throat. It only took a moment, and she was gone—stolen from him and his family.

Could someone have taken James?

God, if I'd given him a damn phone, I could sort this out with a simple call.

"Soph?"

"Huh?" I turn toward Lincoln.

"Who's James?" I swallow past the roughness in my throat and open my mouth to answer him, but nothing comes out. My mouth is so dry, and my tongue feels too big for the space. I lick my lips and swallow. I never told him. I turn back toward my window, my legs shaking up and down with nervous energy. "Sophie?"

I keep my face to the window and whisper, "My son."

The silent car amplifies his sharp intake of breath, but I can't worry about Lincoln right now. I need to find James. He pulls up in front of my home, and I fly out of the car before he comes to a complete stop, heading straight for Dad, who's speaking with two police officers.

His eyes widen when he spots me. "Sophie!" he shouts as he wheels closer. "I-I'm so sorry. This is all my fault." His red, swollen eyes trace over my face with confusion, then move further down my body.

Shit! I'm still dressed for work, and I'm sure the thick eyeliner I wear around my eyes is a smudged mess.

Dad's eyes snap up to something behind me, and his eyes narrow when Linc's hand lands on my lower back. *Double shit!*

A throat clears beside me—"Hello."—and I turn toward the sound. "Ma'am." He tips his head. "I'm Sergeant Grey, and this is Officer Banks. You must be James's mom."

"Yeah. Why are you here and not out looking for my son?" I snap as I wave my arms around like a wild woman.

"We will. We just need a few details from you. The sooner we get detailed information, the sooner we can begin our search."

I nod. *Calm the fuck down. You won't be any help if you go off the damn deep end.* I swipe the wetness from my cheeks that's been constantly streaming down my face since Dad's call. "How can I help?" I hiccup through my tears.

"Your dad couldn't tell us what James was wearing today." He holds his pen poised, ready to take notes.

I describe James's clothing, the color of his hair, height, build, and eye color. His backpack and shoes. Everything I can think of that may help. I dig out my phone and show them my most recent photo of him, and the tears that I'd been holding back while speaking start again like a flood. My body shakes, so I wrap my arms around myself to hold myself together.

"And where have you been this afternoon?"

Puzzled by the sudden question, I stutter. "I-I-I was a-at work." I glance over my shoulder to find Lincoln standing close by, giving me enough space to do what I need to do.

"And where's that?"

I glance at Dad. "*Fine Line Art Studio*."

Officer Banks nods. "The tattoo shop?" I swallow and nod again, too afraid to look at my father. The officer looks across at Lincoln. "And you are?"

"I'm her boss," he tells them as he shoves his hands deep into his pockets.

Sergeant Grey's eyes narrow. "And why are you here?"

I feel the air around Lincoln shift and change as he stands taller. "She was in no condition to drive, so I brought her home."

"Can we please look for my son?" I beg.

"A few more questions, and we'll need some of James's clothing to get a search underway. Can you tell us places he likes to go, about his friends, and whatnot?" I tell the sergeant everything I can think of in my state of panic. "We'll need the contact numbers for his friend's parents." I nod, swallowing down my impatience. I guess the more information they have, the better our chances of finding him, so I tell them everything I can about James.

"All right. I think we have everything. We're going to call this into the station. We'll put out a missing person alert and get a few teams here to help us search the area. He's probably at a friend's house or somewhere equally obvious."

I hope so.

I nod, folding my arms around my body and curling in on myself. Lincoln's arm wraps around my shoulders, and I want to lean into him; to take his strength, but when I glance across at Dad, his face is full of confusion and disappointment, so I step away from the man I need right now. "I need to change so I can search for James." I won't be able to run in these boots, so I race inside without waiting for a response and head straight for my bedroom. I wince when I catch sight of myself in the mirror behind my door. I quickly change into yoga pants and sneakers, then throw on an oversized sweater before tying up my hair in a messy bun. Not much I can do about my face right now. I don't have time to waste cleaning myself up. Too much time has already been wasted.

—lincoln—

SHE HAS A KID.

A kid who's fucking *missing*.

My gut clenches as bile rises, and I grip the back of my neck, squeezing hard to stop my hands from shaking.

Fuck!

She has a kid and never said a damn word.

I've fallen for a woman who has a kid.

I never intended to fall for her.

But I did anyway.

And … she has a damn kid. My vision goes fuzzy around the edges.

A kid that may have been stolen just like Elizabeth was. Now I understand why Sophie was so sick when her dad called, because my gut churns and bile burns its way up my esophagus at the thought of her losing James the way we lost Beth.

I push the sensation down because I can't afford to get lost in the past right now … Sophie needs my support.

She has an eight-year-old son.

My shoulders tense around my ears, and my fists clench at my sides. My heart hammers against my sternum and my blood vibrates through my veins as I come to terms with this reality.

My mind reels, playing the last few months over like a movie, but I can't find any clues that would have given me a warning that Sophie's a mom. I've purposely steered clear of single moms. I didn't want the responsibility. I never wanted to risk falling in love with a woman *and* her kids when something could happen to them. I never wanted the responsibility that came with loving a single mom.

And I've gone and fallen for one, anyway.

I feel completely blindsided.

Fuck!

A throat clears behind me, and I turn, looking down into the angry face of Sophie's father as he scans the tattoos on my arm with heavy disapproval. His narrowed eyes climb back to my face, and he scowls at me. "You have some explaining to do."

I'm not sure what explaining I need to do, but I'm not here to cause trouble. "Look, Mr. Chalmers. I'll tell you whatever you need to know, but we need to find James." I hold my hands up in surrender. "I'm here to help."

His posture softens slightly. "Of course. But don't think we won't be having a chat when this is all sorted out."

Another cop car pulls up, and the officer climbs out. Officer Banks takes James's clothes over to him, and they have a brief discussion.

Sophie leaps down the steps, her swollen eyes flicking from her dad to me and back to him. "Did you check the park?"

"I didn't want to leave in case James came home," he grumbles.

"All right. I'm gonna start there." She turns to me. "Thanks for bringing me home. But I need to get moving."

If she thinks I'd leave her at a time like this, she doesn't know me at all. I step closer, forcing her to tilt her head back to look up at me. "I'm coming with you."

"You don't ha—"

I cut her off and my voice turns to steel. "I'm coming with you. Let's not waste time arguing. Lead the way."

She spins on her heel without another word to me, calling over her shoulder. "I'll call you when we find him. Go inside and stay near your phone."

As we breach the front gate, the cop opens the back door of his cruiser to release a dog. I feel better knowing they're taking this situation as seriously as they are. The cops let the dog sniff James's clothing, then its nose immediately drops to the ground, and the German shepherd moves quickly around the front yard.

Sophie sprints down the sidewalk, and I run to keep alongside her. She told the officer he loves the park, but my gut tells me we won't find him there. We run seven or eight blocks before the park comes into view, and Sophie picks up speed. Panting hard, she lurches through the gate, screaming her son's name. I separate from her and call his name on the opposite side, but I already know he's not here. Kids stop what they're doing and watch as we frantically make our way around the area, checking in tunnels and behind bushes.

A man with a baby strapped to his chest stops me. "What's going on?"

I point across at Sophie. "We're looking for her son, James." I describe him the best I can remember from the description she gave to the police, but before I can finish, the guy's shaking his head.

"Haven't seen a kid matching that description, and we've been here since school finished."

I thank him and head over to Sophie. She swipes at the tears flooding her cheeks when she notices my approach. "I just talked to that guy over there." I point behind me. "He's been here since school got out. He hasn't seen James."

Her chest heaves with exertion, but she nods slowly, her hands rising to her hips. I wish I knew what to say to her, but I'm at a loss. "Okay." Her shoulders rise and fall as she takes in deep breaths and blows each one out. "There's a field where kids play soccer on Monday afternoons about five miles from here. I'll check there."

I know the field she's talking about. It's where we play. "That's a long way for an eight-year-old to walk. Do you really think he'd be there?"

She shrugs and drops her gaze to the grass between us. "I dunno, but I have to try. He's desperate to play soccer, and his friend practices there."

"Fair enough. Let's check it out." She surges forward, but I grab her arm to stop her. "How about we go back to your place and get my car? It'll be easier to go from place to place. Quicker, too."

She nods. "Okay."

I guide her to the gate with my hand on her lower back, and we sprint back to her place, update her dad, collect my car, and head to the soccer field.

Every muscle in my body is tense and maintaining a proper breathing pattern is a struggle, but when I glance at Sophie, I dig deep to find strength I wasn't sure I had. This is bringing back a flood of memories for me.

Memories long buried.

Memories I never wanted to experience again.

I don't know what this means for me ... for *us*. Her having a kid changes things in a way I'm not sure I can handle, but I shove the thoughts away so I can be present. "So, James wants to play soccer?"

She turns her tear-stained face toward me. "Yeah," she murmurs with a shaky breath. "He has to wait while I save enough money to buy him a pair of cleats, but as soon as he can, he'll start playing with some of his friends on Monday afternoon if there's room on their team."

Keeping my eyes on the road, I nod. "I can always help him practice. I play in one of the senior teams down here," I offer as I pull into the parking lot. It's busier than I expected. I'd forgotten the younger teams were having a special open practice session today to encourage new members.

As soon as I pull to a stop, Sophie climbs out of my car, not waiting for me before taking off toward the field. With her hand shielding her eyes against the afternoon sun, she scans the area, and I move beside her. "Send me a photo of James so we can split up."

She glances up at me as though she'd forgotten I was with her. "Uh, sure. Thanks." She quickly sends me a photo and we separate to opposite sides of the field. There are a lot of kids down here; it'll take time to search for him.

I study the photo closely. He has Sophie's dark hair, but his eyes are gray blue and he has a galaxy of freckles across his nose and cheeks. He's a cute kid and I hope he's here somewhere playing with his friends because I can't bear the thought of him being stolen and Sophie having to experience what my family had to go through.

I wander from game to game, dropping my eyes to my phone to keep his image fresh. When I look up again, I spot a boy with dark hair who's wearing the clothes Sophie described to the officers, so I increase my speed to a jog. It's difficult to tell if it's him from this distance, but as I get closer, I'm pretty sure it is.

My heart pounds like it's about to shatter out of my ribcage with excited energy at hopefully finding Sophie's son. When I get close enough, I call out his name, and the boy turns fully in my direction. My relief is instant and overwhelming, and my knees almost buckle as my shoulders sag. He's peering at me with acute distrust, which is good. "James? James Chalmers?"

His eyes narrow and his dark brows scrunch together. "Yeah," he answers, drawing out the word while keeping his distance from me.

"My name's Lincoln. I work with your mom." His features relax. "We've been looking for you."

His head swivels around as he searches for his mom. "Damn. Where is she?"

I look up, spotting her on the opposite side of the field, and point in the direction. "Over there. C'mon, I'll take you to her."

Suspicion clouds his features again. "How mad is she?" He bites his bottom lip, much the way Sophie does when she's unsure of something.

"Bud, she's more worried than mad." I grip his shoulder and squeeze it in reassurance.

A woman steps behind him, eyeing me as she places her hand on his other shoulder, tugging him out of my hold. "Everything okay here, James?"

"Uh, yeah. My mom's looking for me. I gotta go."

Her fingers turn white as she holds him in place, looking at me with distrust. "Look, I don't know who you are, but I'm not letting James go with you. I'll call Sophie and let her know where we are."

My eyebrows shoot up. Pretty sure the woman has James without permission, yet she's being protective of him. I'm torn as to what to do. The woman seems to know Sophie, and James appears to be comfortable with her, so my gut tells me he's safe. "If you wait here, I'll get your mom."

She nods, and I take off in the direction I saw Sophie. When I reach her, I stop in front of her, panting. "Found him." I wave my arm in the direction from where I came. Her eyes widen and I grip her hand, engulfing it in mine. "C'mon."

James is exactly where I left him. Thank fuck.

Sophie disengages from me and bolts the last few yards, dropping to her knees and wrapping her arms around her son, sobbing against him. He stands frozen, his eyes blinking as he scratches his cheek. After a few moments, she pulls back and runs her hands over his body from head to toe. "You're okay. I've been so worried," she sobs.

The woman standing behind James shifts on her feet and twists her fingers together. "Didn't he tell you we were bringing him with us today?"

Sophie looks up at the woman, then drops her eyes back to James, shaking her head. "No, he didn't."

CHAPTER 20

—sophie—

MY BLOOD POUNDS THROUGH MY VEINS AND MY HEART BEATS an erratic rhythm. My head is being cleaved open, and I don't know whether to be mad or relieved as I hold my son. Something I wasn't sure I'd ever do again.

I'm gonna go with relieved and happy that he's okay. I'll be mad later when I can talk to James about pulling stunts like this.

Josh's mom, Elaine, tuts at James and then turns to me. "I'm so sorry. I thought he'd asked permission. I never would have brought him to the open training if I'd known. I can't imagine how worried you've been."

I climb to my feet, keeping James close. "It's not your fault. But I'm gonna take James home. His grandfather is also worried sick." His body stiffens in my hold.

"How mad is Grandad?" He peers up at me, his eyes filled with worry.

"We haven't had time to be mad because we've been too worried."

Elaine grabs James's backpack and holds it out to him. "I understand. I'm so sorry, Sophie." She drops her gaze to

James. "Josh will see you at school tomorrow. Please apologize to your grandad for me. I feel terrible."

I reach forward and squeeze her forearm. "Please don't. You did nothing wrong. I'll talk to you later."

"Aww, Mom. Can't I stay?" James whines, dragging his feet.

"No, James. You can't stay," I snap as I tug him forward. Now that I know he's safe, my anger at his thoughtlessness is taking over.

Lincoln follows behind wordlessly as I wrap my arm around James's shoulders, guiding him to Lincoln's car. We all climb in and I text Dad to let him know we found my wayward son. The car ride home is done in silence and it seems to take forever to drive the five and a half miles. Dad's waiting out the front with a police officer when we arrive. James's eyes widen when he sees the officer, and he turns his attention back to me.

"We had no idea where you were, James. You need to understand that we thought you'd been abducted. The police have been looking for you. We've been worried sick," I tell him as we climb out of the car.

He drops his gaze to the ground but not before I see the shininess in his eyes and the quiver of his lips. "I'm sorry, Mom."

"You need to apologize to Grandad and the policemen. Then I want you to go straight to your room. We need to talk."

He kicks the ground with his shoe. "Yes, Mom." He hangs his head and slumps his shoulders, but makes his way toward Dad.

"I didn't know whether to be mad at him or relieved that he was okay when I saw him. Relief won out, but now I'm so pissed that he scared us like that," I mutter.

Linc wraps his arm around my shoulder and I melt against him, taking the comfort and support he's offering. "Hey, I never met the kid, and I was battling between relieved and pissed. I can't imagine how you're feeling." *He says that, but I'm certain he can.* He drops a kiss to the top of my head and my lids fall closed. "Are you gonna be okay?" he murmurs against my hair. "I can stay or I can leave. Whatever you need, Shortcake."

I wish I could ask him to stay. To help me deal with the fallout from today, but I glance across at Dad, finding him watching us with annoyance. "I think it's best you leave." I reluctantly pull away from the sanctuary of his arms. "James won't be the only one in trouble tonight," I murmur.

Lincoln studies my face closely with curious eyes. "Are you sure you're gonna be okay? Your dad seemed pissed at me … not sure why." He glances over my shoulder and then drops his gaze back to me. "I can stay if you need someone to have your back."

My heart flips at his generous offer, but I need to deal with Dad on my own. We have a lot to discuss, and I think it's going to be a long night. "I'll be fine. I'll see you tomorrow. Hopefully," I whisper the last word under my breath.

He leans down to kiss me, but I turn my face to give him my cheek since Dad's watching us like a hawk.

I'm freaking twenty-six.

I shouldn't let Dad dictate my life choices, but it's tough when I'm still living in his home, and I try—mostly—to be respectful of him and his expectations. Most of the time, he gives me the space to be an adult; however, I don't think I'll have that luxury tonight.

I watch Lincoln leave and apologize profusely to the police officers, then follow Dad and James inside. I lean against the closed door, watching James disappear down the hallway to his bedroom and I know he's genuinely sorry, but it's going to take me a while to recover from this afternoon. I drop my head against the wood, exhausted—emotionally and physically. My muscles are going to be sore tomorrow.

"Sophie Mae?" Shit, he's pulled out the middle name. I

peel my eyes open to find his disapproving glare aimed my way while he waves his arm up and down at me. "I didn't recognize the girl who came home today." His eyes narrow. "I thought all of this was left behind long ago." Wheeling closer, he looks up at me. "And a tattoo shop?" The disappointment dripping from his voice makes me ache, and shame that I couldn't keep living the lie for him when he's done so much for me and James washes through me. "This isn't you."

"This *is* me, Dad," I murmur.

His brows drop over his eyes. Confusion has turned to anger. "No, it isn't. This isn't the daughter I raised on my own." He slams his hand on the arm of his chair. "The daughter I gave everything to."

"I'm sorry I've disappointed you *again*. I've tried." I hold my hands out from my sides. "Lord knows I've tried to be the daughter you want me to be, but I've been struggling to be that person. I need to be me." I swipe at my cheeks while my heart disintegrates in my chest as I utter my truth. "I was dying a little more every day, and I needed to live my life the way I want."

"Not while you're under my roof, you won't. This is the sort of behavior that got you into trouble in the first place,"—I suck in a sharp breath at his blatant accusation—"and I see that you're heading straight down the same road. A-a-and that man." He stabs his finger toward the front door, but he may as well have plunged a dagger into my heart. "With all those … those tattoos. He's clearly more than your boss, Sophie. I may be in a wheelchair with legs that don't work, but my eyes work just fine."

My heart pounds and my body heats. "You know nothing about Lincoln. Don't you dare judge him because of the art he wears on his body," I snap.

"Art," he scoffs. "You know tattoos are the devil's work.

We've had this discussion before!" he shouts, wheeling closer. "I forbid you to see him."

My eyebrows shoot up and I push away from the door, leaning forward to close the distance between us. "He's my boss. You can't forbid me from seeing him. I work for him," I shout back, my blood boiling in my veins.

"You won't be going back there. Find another job!" His hand flies down to his wheel and he spins away from me, rolling down the hallway to the kitchen.

I stomp after him. "I refuse to find another job. I'm finally doing something I love. Something I'm good at." I suck in a sharp breath and dig deep for my bravery. "I love tattoos. I love that my art is going to be on someone's body forever. I love them so much that I … I have tattoos!"

He spins around to face me. "You what!"

I fold my arms across my chest. "*I* have tattoos." I don't know why I'm poking the bear when he's already so angry, but maybe it's time I stopped hiding. "I guess that makes me a terrible person in your eyes, since that's how you judge anyone with a tattoo. That they're somehow less of a person. A troublemaker." I push forward. "And we both know I'm a troublemaker, right? Since I ended up pregnant at seventeen."

I spin on my heel and storm out of the kitchen, not giving him a chance to answer. I don't think my heart can take any more of his disapproval today. When I reach my bedroom, I slam my door like an angry teen. Maybe it's time James and I moved out. I can't live my life to keep him happy while slowly withering away to nothing.

I've felt more like myself since I started working with Lincoln and Ken than I have in a long time and I don't want to give that up but I may have to. I have some savings, but it won't last long and my wage won't be enough to support us if we have to pay rent too. I flop back on my bed and let my angry tears fall. I know I need to speak with James about what he did today, but I need to think and regroup first.

I brush my wet hair over my shoulder and knock on James's door.

"Come in."

I step inside and close the door behind me, finding James sitting on the window seat with his legs pulled up beneath his chin.

Without lifting his head, he looks up at me. "I'm sorry, Mom. Josh told me his mom could take me to the special training session with them today. I was gonna tell Grandad, but then he wasn't waiting at the bus stop and I had to walk home … and then he was asleep and I … I couldn't. And then I was gonna write a note to tell you guys where I was, but Josh's mom turned up and I didn't have time … and then I left … and I shouldn't have done that. I'm so sorry. Please don't stop me from playing soccer. And it wasn't Josh's mom's fault. I shoulda written the note." Tears track down his freckle-covered cheeks. "And now you and Granddad are fighting and it's all my fault."

I take the few steps I need to get to him. "We weren't fighting about you." I sit next to him and brush his hair out of his face. "He's mad at me."

He looks up at me with shimmering eyes. "Are we gonna have to move out? I heard Grandad say *not while you're under my roof* and it sounded like he doesn't want us here anymore."

Wrapping my arm around him, I pull him in close. "Sometimes adults say things they don't mean when they're angry but he never said he wanted us to leave. He just doesn't want me to work in a tattoo studio. I was disrespectful, James. I knew he wouldn't like me working there, but I did it anyway and then I hid it from him."

I'm a terrible mother and an awful role model—sneaking behind Dad's back. What sort of message does that send James?

"Why did you do it?" He presses against me further and I lean down to kiss his head.

I exhale a long breath and shrug. "It's something I've always wanted to do. I love tattoos and the idea of decorating someone's skin with my art … well … to me … it's the perfect way to use my talent. I don't want my drawings and designs to be stuck on someone's wall, I want them to *mean* something. I know Grandad doesn't like tattoos and he thinks they're bad—"

Creases appear between his eyebrows. "Then why are you doing it if you know Grandad doesn't like them?"

"When I was a kid, I always tried to do everything"—*well, mostly everything*—"Grandad wanted but as an adult, I can't always do that." Lord knows I've tried. "Anyway, enough about me. I came in here to talk to you about today. You know what you did wasn't okay, right?"

His chin drops, stealing his eyes from me. "I know." He snaps his head back up. "Maybe you should get me a pho—"

"Don't finish that sentence. I've discussed this with you. You're not getting a phone."

"But if I had a phone, I could have called you at work and told you where I was. Then none of this would have happened." He huffs, folding his arms across his slender frame.

That was one of my thoughts when I was panicking about where he was, but another phone isn't in the budget and definitely won't be a possibility if we move out. "Josh's mom has a phone. You could have asked her to call me. I don't think the phone is the issue here. The issue is you making arrangements without discussing it with me first."

"You weren't home. How can I *discuss*"—he widens his eyes as if to punctuate his sassy attitude—"it with you?"

"Watch your tone with me, James. You were in the wrong today and you know it as well as I do." He opens his mouth, but I shake my head. "New rule. Any plans must be approved by me at least twenty-four hours in advance. No more making last-minute arrangements."

He jumps up from the window seat. "Aw, Mom. That's not fair. Sometimes my friends do stuff after school that we talked about at lunch." His little fists slam into his hips. "Like today."

"Twenty-four hours!" I snap.

Turning his back to me, his shoulders slump. "That's not fair. I'm not gonna be able to do anything anymore. None of my friends will want to be my friend because I can't join in. I'll get left out of everything." He pouts, and guilt that I'm being too hard on him threatens to swallow me whole, but I refuse to go through what we went through this afternoon ever again.

Standing, I wrap my arms around him from behind and kiss the top of his head. "I'm sorry, James. This is how it has to be."

"What if I promise to always leave a note?"

I shake my head. I'll give him points for trying. "Not happening. Now get started on your homework while I cook dinner. I'll see you in the kitchen in thirty minutes."

CHAPTER 21

—lincoln—

I SLEPT LIKE SHIT LAST NIGHT—WORRY FOR SOPHIE AND JAMES had me tossing and turning, reinforcing exactly why I've avoided single moms all these years. I gave up on trying to sleep around five and climbed out of bed, made a coffee, and have been sitting on my back porch watching the world wake up. With rose and golden hues painted across the sky, I contemplate what to do about Sophie. I listen to Aaron move about and leave for work while I ruminate over everything I learned yesterday.

She's everything I've tried to avoid and yet she's perfect—even if she comes with my worst nightmare … *a kid.*

I have nothing against kids, it's just that I never wanted the responsibility. I'm shit at keeping them safe, and I don't think my heart's strong enough when something inevitably happens.

And something will always happen. It's unavoidable.

I was crawling out of my skin as we searched for James—a kid I'd never met. How will I cope if something happens to him once I've gotten to know him and wrapped him in my love?

Watching Sophie fall apart and drag her pieces back

together so she could find her son was one of the most inspiring and terrifying moments I've witnessed. She was so fucking strong in a situation that would have had most people —me in particular—crumbling to dust.

I go for my morning run, shower, make a protein smoothie, and head over to Sophie's, since her car is still at work. When I pull up in front of her house, knowing she lives here with her dad and son, I see it through different eyes.

Shaking my head, I still can't believe she has a kid, and I think it'll take a while for me to wrap my head around it.

I'm guessing that's why she's had such a long dry spell.

I know I'm early, but I'm hoping we can talk before work, so I climb the steps and knock on the front door. After a moment, movement catches my eye through the glass side panel. The door opens, and Sophie's dad rolls forward.

On top of his worry for James, he seemed pissed yesterday. "Sophie won't be working for you anymore. Have a good day." He wheels back and grips the door, pushing it closed, but I step inside; preventing it and his eyes widen at my brazenness.

I hold up my hands. "I'm going to need Sophie to tell me she no longer works for me."

"I'm her father and *I'm* telling you," he splutters as his eyes drag down my tattoos and I get the impression he isn't a fan.

"And I said, I need to hear it from her. Last I checked, she's an adult who can make her own decisions." I lift my eyes from her dad and scan what I can see of their home—photos line the wall of a young family and I recognize Sophie as a toddler and young girl—but I can't hear any other sounds in the house. "Please tell her I'm here to take her to work."

His eyes narrow, and his spine straightens. "She's not here. She had to take James to the bus for school since she left her car at work."

"No problem. I'll wait for her." I close the door behind me and stroll into the living room, taking a seat. Where there would normally be a recliner, the space is void of any furniture, I assume to allow space for the wheelchair.

"I didn't invite you into my home," he sputters, rolling into the room behind me. "You're not our kind of people. I'm not sure what my daughter was thinking when she applied for a job at a tattoo studio." He scoffs. "I'd already forbidden her from working at *artWORX*." He waves his arm in the air dismissively and my eyebrows rise halfway up my forehead.

Forbid?

Does he realize she's an adult, and he has no control over what she does?

"Why would you *forbid* her? She's an incredibly talented artist and an adult who is more than capable of making her own decisions."

He huffs. "I can't trust her to make sensible decisions. Look what happened when she was left to her own devices. She got pregnant at seventeen by that boy at her prom." He rolls closer with narrowed eyes. "Then she worked at that tattoo shop and the boss tried to molest her." Anger boils in my veins when I think about Barry. "And here we go again. Another poor decision that she knew I wouldn't like, so she snuck around behind my back!" he sputters, his face red with anger.

"Dad!" Sophie's voice snaps out like a whip and she looks from him to me and back again with wide eyes. "Stop already!" When she looks back at me, her eyes are shiny. I know her well enough to see she's holding back tears. "Linc, what are you doing here?"

I stand, jamming my hands into my pockets, and rock back on my heels. I almost don't recognize her. Her face is makeup-free, and she's wearing a yellow sundress that brings out the cinnamon highlights in her long hair. She looks beautiful. "I came to drive you to work, since your car is still there. I figured you'd need a ride."

She smiles shakily, her eyes flicking from me to her father. "Thank you. I'll grab my stuff."

Her dad rolls forward, all bluster. "You will not. I *forbid* you, Sophie." There's that fucking word again. I step forward and he glances at me with angry eyes. "If you leave this house with him, don't come back!"

Sophie freezes, and the tears she was holding at bay fall over her thick, dark lashes. "You don't mean that," she whispers shakily.

He nods sharply, his face red. "I do."

I step between father and daughter. "Sir, I don't think you want to do that. I can see you love Sophie and James and you only want what's best for them, but I don't think giving her an ultimatum is the answer."

"Mind your own business. This doesn't concern you."

I advance, then feel Sophie's small hand grip my T-shirt. "With all due respect, Sir. If it involves Sophie, it *does* concern me. She's not only my employee, she's my future." Until that moment, my mind was jumbled about what to do with my feelings for Sophie. As her father speaks to her like a child, my decision is made. And it feels … *right*. Her gasp rings loudly behind me, and her fingers tighten in the cotton she's gripping. "She and James are my priority, and I won't allow anyone to disrespect either of them—even if that person is you. They can live with me if you're intent on kicking them out. It's up to you, Mr. Chalmers." I hold out my hands, non-threateningly.

Damn, I'm making shit up as I go now.

My mind races through potential solutions. Aaron and I have a room we can turn into a bedroom for James, but I probably should check if it's okay with him first.

I wanted to take her to breakfast to talk about her being a single mom and what that would mean for our relationship moving forward. Instead, I've invited her and her son to move into my home without consulting my best friend.

Everything's moving faster than I had planned, but I'm gonna roll with it.

Sophie releases her grip on my T-shirt and steps out from behind me. "That won't be necessary,"—she drops her gaze to the floor—"I'll find somewhere for me and James to live."

"Soph—" her dad whispers.

Sadness washes through the room with the shake of her head. "It's time we moved out, anyway. You can't respect my need for me to be me. I wish it hadn't come to this, but I'm twenty-six, and I need to live my life without being held back." She sucks in a shaky breath. "I'm sorry I couldn't live up to your expectations, but I think it's time."

She turns on her ballet flats and leaves us in the living room. I chance a look at her dad to find him wiping beneath his eyes with trembling fingers. "She's so much like her mother," he murmurs. "Such a damn spitfire." He slumps in his chair. "I can't lose her and James. They're all I have left," he murmurs. Silence falls heavy between us, but I don't feel the need to fill it.

With an air of pride, Sophie returns several minutes later wearing the Dr. Martens I made her keep on the other night, denim shorts that expose her thigh tattoo, a burgundy crop top, messy hair, red-painted lips, and thick black eyeliner around her stunning eyes.

This is the Sophie I recognize.

I'm not sure which version of her is *her* truth, but I'm equally attracted to both versions. Her father gasps but stays rooted to the spot—his eyes stuck on her thigh tattoo—as she grabs her purse, then turns toward him.

"Can you please collect James from the bus this afternoon? He's starting summer vacation next week. I'll work something out so we aren't reliant on you, but I'd appreciate your help today." Her shoulders drop a little. "I'm sorry I've disappointed you, Dad. I want you to know that I tried to squash the real me so I could make you proud, but I was slowly dying inside. It has never been my intention to deceive or hurt you; I was just doing my best to keep you happy." I watch her throat bob as she twists her fingers together. "I love you, Dad."

She turns, hiding her face, but not before I notice her tears. I step forward to join her when her dad holds up his hand to stop me.

"Sophie," he says, his voice softer than I've heard. He wheels closer to her and takes her hand in his, stroking his thumb across her knuckles. "I'm sorry. I responded poorly a-a-and I sometimes forget that you're not my little girl anymore. That you're a grown woman,"—he gives her a watery smile and I watch her soften—"and you can make your own choices. I sometimes forget that I need to let you go … to find your own sense of self. To find your own path. I-I know I can occasionally be controlling and stifling,"—Sophie blinks quickly and raises her eyebrows at her dad—"okay, maybe more than occasionally." He chuckles. "But it comes from a place of love. You and James are all I have and I want to keep you safe." *I hear ya, man!* "Please don't move out. This is your home and you'll always have a place here. I-I-I'll work on tempering my ways. I love you, Sophie. Please don't leave."

She bends down to him, and they wrap each other in a tight embrace which they hold for long moments, her body shuddering. She pulls away with a sniffle. "Thank you, Dad. We'll stay if you think you can accept me for who I am. I promise this doesn't make me a bad person. I'm still your Sophie." He's nodding before she finishes her sentence. "I'm not giving up my job. I love it too much." He nods again. "If I'm going to be a good role model for James, he needs to see me following my passion. He needs to see me being authentic to myself. I don't want him to fit into a box. I want him to know it's okay to be himself."

"I know," he says, his voice dripping with regret. "I'm

sorry." He turns to me. "I still want to have a chat with you, young man." His voice is full of sharp edges when he addresses me.

I hold out my hands. "Any time. And if you'd like to come down and check out the studio to ease your worry, you're welcome to do that too."

"Thank you. I'll take you up on that. Now you two had better get moving, or you'll be late and I need to get this next chapter written."

Sophie leans back down to hug her dad goodbye and we head out to my car.

—sophie—

I EXHALE A HEAVY BREATH WHEN I SINK INTO THE LEATHER OF Lincoln's front seat. It's been an emotionally exhausting sixteen hours, and I'd prefer to curl up in a ball on my bed and hide beneath the covers. Alas, grown-ups can't do stuff like that.

I'm too scared to look at Lincoln. I can't believe he stood up to Dad and told him I'm his future. That James and I are his future like his words were of no consequence. Surely he didn't mean it. They were just words said in the heat of the moment. Right?

He starts the engine and I'm waiting for him to break the silence, but he doesn't. I steal a glance his way, tracing my eyes from his hand casually draped over the steering wheel, along his arm with that amazing geometric tattoo, to his bicep which tenses. I continue my path upwards, tracing my eyes over the chain he has around his neck and further up his throat. I watch his Adam's apple bob as he swallows, and graze my teeth on my bottom lip as I remember how his scruff-covered cheeks felt against the inside of my thighs.

He's so freaking hot. But he's also strong and loyal. Supportive and wonderfully kind.

He turns his gaze toward me and gives me a panty-melting smile—causing crinkles at the corners of his eyes to show—which quickly falls along with his eyebrows. "Are you okay?"

"Did you mean what you said?"

Creases form between his brows, and he glances back at the road. "Which part?"

I swallow and dig deep for my bravery. He said it, so I'm not sure why I'm nervous about bringing it up. "About me and James … and … and your future?"

He switches his hands on the steering wheel and reaches across to grip one of mine, dragging it across to rest on his firm thigh. "Well, yeah. I didn't mean to blurt it out in front of your dad. I was hoping we could talk about things this morning before work." He pulls into a parking lot that isn't the one behind the studio. I narrow my eyes when I realize he's pulled into a café next to the river. Without another word, he climbs out and opens my door, holding his hand out for me to take. "Let's eat and we can talk."

With our fingers entwined, he walks inside like he owns the place and heads straight toward the doors that sound like they lead to the kitchen. As soon as they open, the noise level doubles as pans clatter and people call out instructions. I tug on Linc's hand. "I don't think we're supposed to be in here."

He glances at me. "Nah, we're good." He looks around the busy kitchen and tugs me forward. "Aaron! Make us some breakfast, will ya?" he calls.

I immediately recognize his friend when he turns around. His eyes drop to where our hands are linked, and he raises a single eyebrow as he makes his way back up to Lincoln's face.

He walks toward us, wiping his hands on a towel as he chuckles. "Sophie! Great to see you again." He leans in to hug me, but Lincoln tugs me back, causing his friend to laugh louder. "I see how it is. Go sit out front; I'll make you a couple of breakfast wraps." He turns to me. "Anything you don't eat?"

Shaking my head, I answer. "I'm not fussy and don't have any allergies. Thank you." My stomach chooses that moment to gurgle. I was still so upset about everything that happened yesterday that I hadn't been able to stomach the thought of breakfast and I barely touched my dinner last night. None of us did, and I wondered why I'd even bothered to cook.

The guys chuckle and Lincoln tugs me out of the kitchen, between the patrons, toward an empty table by the window. The view is stunning and I take a moment to appreciate the glassiness of the water beneath the clear, blue sky. A few people are rowing, leaving ripples in the water, while water birds fly overhead. I blow out a long breath, uncoiling my muscles as the tension releases. "It's gorgeous here." I lower myself into the chair Lincoln pulls out for me and look up at him. "Thank you."

We're both silent, our eyes trained out of the window until our wraps arrive, and we dig into the tasty breakfast. I wait patiently for Lincoln to start the conversation we need to have, unease dripping down my spine. He finally finishes eating and then locks his arresting blue eyes on me. The same blue eyes that stare at me from the tattoo on his arm. "Is there a reason you never mentioned you had a kid?"

My eyebrows shoot up. I'm not sure what I was expecting, but I didn't expect that to be his first question and I also didn't expect to hear the hurt in his voice. Taking a moment to gather my thoughts, I sip my coffee and then wipe my mouth. "I never mentioned James because I could just be me. It's been a long time since I've done something just for me,"—I swallow nervously. *Is he going to think I'm selfish?*—"and it's made me feel more like myself than I have in years. At work, I wasn't someone's mom or daughter. I was just me … and I liked it. I didn't want to lose that feeling." I shift in my seat. "I didn't think my parental status had any bearing on my work."

He nods slowly, his eyes softening. "I get that, and you

being a mom doesn't impact your job." He looks away for a moment, then locks his eyes onto mine. "But it affects our relationship." My heart skips to a stop. *Relationship?* I … my mind races and it shouldn't because he just told my father that James and I are his future. He leans forward, resting his arms on the table, and sighs loudly. "I've avoided single moms, Sophie," he breathes. "There's no other way to say it. I didn't want kids. I never wanted the responsib—"

I stiffen in my seat. "I never asked you to take responsibility for James. I expect nothing from you." I lean forward and lower my voice. "Just because we slept together, I don't expect you to ride in on your white horse and rescue us. We've been doing fine on our own. We don—"

He holds up his hand. "Woah! Stop for a second." My chest heaves with angry breaths. "Let me finish, please." He raises his dark brows, waiting for me to agree. I nod slightly, and he jams his fingers through his messy waves. "As I was saying. I never wanted the responsibility of keeping them safe. It's too fucking hard … and I'm shit at it." Pain laces every word, causing fissures to split across my heart, making it ache for the boy who *still* thinks he failed his sister. When he first told me about her, I could taste his despair in the air. I imagine he had to grow up fast because of what happened. My heart breaks for the boy and aches for the man who's lost so much. I slide my hand over his, lacing our fingers together. "I never wanted to have my heart broken like that. I never wanted to fall for a woman *and* her kid only to have something happen. I wouldn't survive the devastation."

"Oh, Linc." I'll never know why I ever thought this man was an angry storm—he just feels so deeply. But now I'm worried the relationship I didn't realize we had might be over before it's begun because of this deep-seated belief that he's responsible for his sister's disappearance.

"But I couldn't help it. I fell for you … so fucking hard, and while I should run in the opposite direction, I find I can't. My feet are rooted here … next to you. Next to you *and* your son." His eyes bore into mine and a dark chuckle huffs past his lips. "I don't even know him, but I know I'm gonna fall for him as hard as I've fallen for you. I didn't stand a chance. As soon as our hands made contact at the interview, I was gone."

My heart tries to leap from behind my ribs to beat with his and I would give anything to be in private right now so I can climb into his lap and wrap myself around him. Soothe him *and* his fears. Tell him I've fallen for him too and if he's prepared to risk his heart, I'll care for it and keep it safe.

"Lincoln," I murmur. "The one thing I've learned so far in my life is that there are no guarantees … for anyone. As much as I wish I could lay your fears to rest, I don't know what's in the future." I lean closer. "But here's the tea … living in fear of *what if* is a lonely place to be. It means you don't take risks. You don't grow to your full potential. You miss out. And worst of all, you don't love with your whole heart." I reach out to lay my hand over his pounding heart. "And you have such a big heart, Linc. It would be a shame to waste it."

He shakes his head and one side of his mouth tips up as his eyes crawl over my face. "How did you get so wise?"

I raise and drop one shoulder. "I wouldn't say I'm wise." I grin. "I remember a time when you thought I'd turn out to be flaky." I raise a single brow.

He chuckles. "How wrong I was …"—he covers my hand resting on the pec over his heart—"about so many things. I don't want to miss out, Shortcake. Not anymore."

Leaning forward, I lightly press my lips to his. "You don't have to. I promise to help you through your fears and worries."

-epilogue-

—lincoln—

"Are you sure you want me to do this?" Sophie asks, disbelief etched into her gorgeous face.

I nod once. "One hundred percent."

Her throat bobs as she swallows. Tension still brackets her mouth. "What if I mess it up?"

"You won't."

"But what if I do?" I don't think I've ever seen my Shortcake so unsure of herself.

"You won't."

Her leg shakes up and down. "How can you be so sure?"

"Because I know how important it is to you to do the best work you can. I've watched you working on the fake skin and you've perfected your technique. You haven't messed up a single tattoo for our clients so far." I cup her cheek. "And I have faith in you." Leaning in, I press my lips to hers because I can't resist when I'm this close. I spent too long resisting her, and I refuse to do it now that I don't have to.

"Okay, okay, you two. Enough already," Ken playfully admonishes.

I tear my eyes from Sophie to look at Ken. "She's nervous."

He freezes with his watering can perched in the air. "What are you nervous about, doll?"

"I don't wanna mess it up." She waves her hand around my body. "All of his artwork is stunning. It's a little intimidating."

He chuckles. "Well, that's because I've done it all. But your work is equally stunning. All the pieces you've done have been breathtaking."

"They've been small pieces, Ken. This … this is different. It's bigger." She bites her bottom lip. "Will you fix it if I mess it up?" she asks.

"Sure, doll, but I won't need to do shit." Finished with the conversation because he knows as well as I do that Sophie's work will be perfect, he returns to his task of watering the plants.

She looks up at me, uncertainty still warring in her eyes. "Do it!" I mouth.

Picking up the gun, she presses it against my bicep, and with one last flick of her eyes to mine, the machine hums to life. Her focus is absolute, and it's sexy as hell. I relax into the pressure, keeping my eyes on her as she works.

The doorbell sounds and I spot James holding the door open and then his grandad rolls through. They've been catching the bus across town once a week to visit since Sophie's secret came to light. The first time they came, James bolted inside, shouting out for Sophie. Because she's an awesome mom; she greeted him with love and then promptly explained he needs to be quiet and respectful when he enters so as not to startle anyone. He's such a great kid that he apologized to everyone and has been on his best behavior ever since.

She's so focused on what she's doing that she's unaware that her family's here. I told her dad that she was going to tattoo me this afternoon and it would be a great opportunity for him to see his daughter's talent firsthand, so I'm happy to see that he came.

She lifts the gun from my bicep. "Stop twitching," she admonishes me.

"James and your dad are here," I murmur with a raised brow, lifting my chin toward the door.

Her eyes widen and she spins on her stool. "James. Dad." She places her gun on the trolley and heads over to greet them.

When she releases James, he comes directly to me with wide eyes. "Mom's tattooing you?"

I ruffle his hair and pull him into me with a chuckle. "Sure is, bud. I couldn't have everyone else wearing her art and not have some of it for myself."

"That's so cool." His eyes trace every line and curve with interest.

Trevor rolls over to us. He's still not one hundred percent comfortable with Sophie working here, but his prejudice against people with tattoos has diminished somewhat. "Lincoln." He dips his chin at me and I take a few steps to him to shake his hand.

"Mr. Chalmers. Good to see you."

"You too."

He points to my arm. "Is that Sophie's artwork?"

I look down at the new lines, not that I need to, but I'll probably spend a lot of time looking at it because it's Sophie's. "Yep. She drew this design on me with a pen a while back when she was practicing. I loved it so much that I want it permanently on my skin."

He clears his throat as his eyes skim the detailed design. "It's very good."

I glance up at Sophie in time to see her hand fly to her mouth and her eyes soften. Her shoulders drop from around her ears; something I've noticed happens every time her dad enters my studio. "She's extremely talented." I walk over to the table where we normally meet with clients and grab Sophie's portfolio. "Here are photos of the work she's done so far. Some of the early pieces are her designs, but my work, the more recent images show Sophie's work from start to finish."

He slowly rolls closer as if I'm holding a grenade, not a folder of artwork. I move a chair away so he can sit at the table and then sit beside him. When I open the first page to an image of Natasha's breasts, he flinches. "I don't need to see a woman's breasts. That's private."

"Oh, don't worry about that. Natasha's happy to have the image in Sophie's portfolio. She's incredibly proud of the artwork Soph designed for her." I glance up at Sophie as she moves closer.

"She's a survivor of breast cancer," I explain.

"Oh, that's terrible," Trevor says, his tone dripping with sincerity.

"Cancer stole a lot from her. It left her scarred and her self-esteem in ruins. She hated seeing her reflection in the mirror. Natasha heard I specialize in tattooing women who have survived breast cancer, so she came in to claim back her body."

Sophie sits in the chair on the opposite side of her father and looks at me. "Not only specializes,"—she looks at her dad —"he does them for free because his mom is a breast cancer survivor."

Trevor's eyes soften when he looks back at me. "That's a very noble thing to do, Lincoln."

Warmth spreads through my body, and my chest feels light. "Thank you. It's the least I can do after the battle they've faced. If I can help them recover some of their self-worth, then I'm happy to help."

Sophie rests her hand over her dad's. "You should have seen the difference in Natasha from when she walked in here to when she walked out." Her eyes grow glassy. "She was a different person. And her husband … he was so thankful that his wife could have that piece of herself back."

Trevor's eyes drop to the photograph and I watch him

studying it closely. He raises his head and nods. "The artwork is very beautiful, sweetie. I'm glad you could help her."

I watch Sophie's throat move as her lips tip up in a tremulous smile. "Thanks, Dad. That means a lot to me."

"I want a tattoo, Mom."

Sophie's head snaps up toward her son and she narrows her eyes. "No tattoos for you until you're at least twenty-one."

"Awwww, Mom. That's not fair."

Trevor looks at me with a smirk. "Good luck taming that boy." A laugh huffs past my lips. "He's a lot like his mother and grandmother." He winks. "Wild ones. All three of them."

CHAPTER 24

—sophie—

L INCOLN CONGRATULATES THE BOYS AS THEY RUN OFF THE FIELD after winning their game. Every time James and Lincoln bond over soccer, my heart expands to the point I'm worried it might burst. I think James will always remember this summer vacation because Lincoln spent most mornings before we left for work teaching him the basic skills he needed to play the game. Because of all that time together, they've grown incredibly close. They high-five each other and make their way over to Dad and me with matching grins.

"You have a good man there, Sophie. I'm sorry I judged him so harshly." He grips my hand. "Please accept my apology."

I lean down and kiss his cheek. "Apology accepted, but you're apologizing to the wrong person."

"Mom! Grandad! Did you see my goal? It was awesome!"

I chuckle as he leaps at me. "I sure did. I'm so proud of you!" I kiss his sweaty forehead and he squeezes me tight, then releases me to receive congratulations from Dad. Lincoln wraps his arms around me from behind, and I cover his hands with mine, tangling our fingers together as we watch James recount every second of his incredible goal to Dad as if he weren't watching for himself.

"He played well this afternoon."

I lean my head back against Lincoln's firm chest with contentment filling my heart. "Thanks to you." I tilt my head back to look up at him and he kisses my forehead.

I feel him shrug. "I enjoy hanging out with him. He's a great kid. You've done a great job with him."

"Thank you." I spin around and press up on my toes to kiss his cheek. "He loves hanging out with you. He's missed out on having someone he can play outside with."

"I'm hungry, Mom."

I chuckle and step out of Lincoln's arms. "All right. Let's grab dinner, so Lincoln can come back in time for his game."

"Can I watch tonight?" James asks with wide, excited eyes. We've been grabbing dinner and coming back to watch Lincoln play during school vacation, but that's over now.

I tap his nose. "Nope. It's a school night."

He kicks the grass with his cleat. "Awww. That's not fair."

"Yeah, well, a lot of things aren't fair. Let's go." He bends to grab his sports bag and Lincoln pushes Dad across the grass to the parking lot.

As he pulls up to our house, I notice the real estate agent placing a sold sticker on the sign in front of the house that's been vacant for ages across the road. Lincoln parks and we climb out of the car, then he helps Dad out of the front seat and into his wheelchair.

"I wonder what our new neighbors will be like?" I muse out loud.

Dad and Lincoln glance at each other, then focus on the house across the street. "I hope they're decent, community-minded people." He glances up at Lincoln with raised brows.

"I'm sure they will be, Mr. Chalmers," he responds, winking at Dad.

Sometimes I have to pinch myself that Dad has put his prejudice aside to welcome Lincoln into our family. Over the last few months, I've often found them talking about their losses and how they each blame themselves—something I had no idea Dad did. My heart fractured when I overheard him explaining to Lincoln that if he hadn't had an appointment with his publisher across town, we never would have been on that train.

After Lincoln shared the loss of his sister and the subsequent breakdown of his parent's marriage as a result, Dad seems to have taken him under his wing. I think their budding relationship has been great for both of them, and Dad's acceptance of my job and relationship with Lincoln has meant I haven't had to sneak around.

"Okay, James. I want you to wash up while I start dinner." He drops his sports bag on the floor and peels away from us. "Hey, take your bag with you so you can sort it out."

He freezes and spins around. "Sorry, Mom. I'm starving and forgot." He grabs his bag and disappears down the hallway.

Lincoln chuckles quietly behind me. "He's a lot like me, thinking of his stomach." He kisses the top of my head while he wraps his arm around my waist, and I sink into him, just as I do every time he's near. "Hope you don't mind, but I ordered Italian delivery because there's something I need to show you."

My stomach flips. "Any time I don't have to make dinner, I'm happy." I turn in his hold, press my hands to his pecs, and stand on my tiptoes to kiss his cheek. "What do you need to show me?"

He grabs my hand and turns to Dad. "Won't be long."

"Take your time. We're not going anywhere."

He drags me outside, excitement bubbling from him. He's lighter than I've ever seen, and I love seeing this side of him. With Lincoln, I feel like I learn unique parts of him all the time. I giggle, swept up in his obvious joy as we leap down the front steps and he drags me across the road to the vacant house.

Confusion creeps in as we come to a stop in front of the sold sign. "What's going on?"

He turns to face me, collecting my other hand, then inhales sharply and exhales a harsh breath. Worry has replaced some of his happiness. "I have something to ask you. Well, you and James, but I wanted to ask you first." He glances at the house we're standing in front of. "I know we started on shaky ground, but I realized pretty early on that I'd fallen for you. It … this …"—he waves his hand between us—"you were completely unexpected. You showed me everything I'd been missing because of my fears. I've learned to accept that I wasn't responsible for what happened the day Beth went missing and even though I can't guarantee that I won't slip back into old thought patterns, I feel emotionally stronger and more capable of accepting that life comes with risks. And that's thanks to you, Soph."

I squeeze his hands and blink quickly to prevent the sting of tears from falling down my cheeks. I lose the battle as one breaks through, followed by another. My lips tremble as I try to smile.

He releases my hands to wipe my cheeks. "Don't cry, Shortcake."

"I can't help it; I fell for you, too," I whisper as he cups my cheeks.

He leans down and presses his lips softly to mine. "Good to know." When he pulls away, he winks at me. "But I wanted to tell you I've fallen in love with you." My heart gallops wildly, thumping around in my chest cavity and my knees turn to Jell-O and when I open my mouth, he shakes his head, pressing his thumb over my lips. "I was wondering if you and James would like to move in with me …here?" He tips his head toward the empty house.

My eyes blow wide and my mouth drops open. I glance at the house, then back to Lincoln in astonishment. "Are you serious?" That's quite the turnaround for someone who didn't want to have anything to do with a single mom.

"I've never been more serious." He tilts my face up to his. "I've given it a lot of thought and I can't picture a future without you and James in it. I don't see the point of wasting time when I know what I want, and that's for us to be a family. I want us to live together, to create a family home. When this house came onto the market, I thought it would be perfect because it means we can still help your Dad. James can come and go between the two houses after school. It seemed a perfect fit for us, even though it needs some work."

I open and close my mouth. "I-I-I don't know what to say." I glance back at the house and then up at the man who consumes my every thought.

"Say yes!" Dad shouts from across the street and I snap my head around, finding him at the front gate, smiling widely.

Lincoln squeezes my hands, bringing my attention back to him. "Out of respect for your dad, I had to ask him if he was okay with this."

I chuckle. "I'd say he's on board with your plan."

"The only person I really need to be on board with my plan is you. Please say yes, Soph."

"As if I would say anything else. YES!" A startled laugh bursts out of me when he scoops me into his arms and spins me around, my legs flying out behind me.

Applause rings out from across the road as Lincoln slams his mouth onto mine and once I catch up to what's happening, I tangle my fingers through his hair and return his kiss with enthusiasm. Opening my mouth, I stroke his tongue with mine as I wrap my legs around his hips. With every lick and sigh, I fall a little more in love. His hands drop to my ass, supporting me, and I'm mildly aware that we're moving, but I don't care where he takes me, as long as he never stops kissing me.

Loving me.

Shit, I haven't told him I love him.

Using my grip on his hair, I drag his mouth away from mine and press my forehead to his. "I love you, Lincoln Kingsley. So much. I can't wait to start our life together."

Dear Reader,

Thank you so much for reading Wicked Kisses.

I'm a reader and an author who loves to read and write stories that have all the threads neatly tied up in a bow. However, for this story, there is a thread that I purposely left unraveled.

This book was originally part of the charity anthology, The Trouble with Bad Boys. *The purpose of the anthology was to raise money for* Operation Underground Railroad, *a charity that supports victims of human trafficking, so I incorporated it into my story. Every day, all around the world, organized groups steal women and children from their lives for financial gain.*

Their families don't get closure.

They never—or rarely—find out what happened to their loved ones.

They don't know where they are or if they're alive or dead.

Families and friends live their lives with unanswered questions and an empty place in their shattered hearts.

… and so I left Elizabeth's storyline open. I hope you understand.

Her family has no answers and neither do we.

xo Debra

Would you like a sneak peek into the future?
Sign up for my newsletter to find out how Lincoln reacts when he and
Sophie learn something unexpected.
https://tinyurl.com/wickedkisses-bonus

Are you ready to meet Lincoln's friend, Max, in **Moonlit Kisses?**
An age-gap workplace romance
A steamy, low-angst, stand-alone contemporary romance about
a workaholic mechanic with a generous heart fighting his
attraction to his assistant, and a younger woman who's down
on her luck but never gives in or gives up.
https://books2read.com/dsj-moonlitkisses

Lincoln's soccer friend and the owner of Brady's Pub, Finn Brady, meets his match in **Enemy Kisses**.
An enemies to lovers romance novella
A steam-filled, angsty, stand-alone contemporary romance about a misunderstood pub owner who has no problem working for the affections of his brand-new neighbor and the baker who tries her best to guard her heart but isn't able to fight the tempting pull of her enemy.
https://books2read.com/dsj-enemykisses

pinterest

I put together a Pinterest board for Lincoln and Sophie's story. If you're interested, you can check it out here:

https://tinyurl.com/wickedkisses-pinterest

connect with debra

stalk me

You can stalk me pretty much everywhere!
https://debrastjamesbooks.com/connect/

How about joining my Facebook group?
https://www.facebook.com/groups/DebsBibliomaniacs

newsletter

Join Debra's newsletter to receive important updates before anyone else. Newsletters will be sent once a month unless something exciting is happening.
https://debrastjamesbooks.com/newsletter/

thank you

Thank you so much for reading Lincoln and Sophie's story. This story was an interesting challenge for me. It was originally part of the charity anthology, *The Trouble with Bad Boys*, with the theme *'bad boys'*. As you know, I write cinnamon roll Heroes, so I was a little daunted, but I desperately wanted to support the charity—*Operation Underground Railroad*! Hence, a misunderstood Hero who appeared to be a bad boy, but was really a cinnamon roll in disguise.

As always, I would like to thank Mr. St James and our two sons for their support and patience with me. My writing takes a lot of my time away from my family and their understanding and support is always appreciated.

To my alpha reader, Rachel and her hubby for seeking and pointing out my Aussie-isms and giving me valuable feedback. To my beta readers, Kelly, Wendy, and Kelly, thank you for your invaluable feedback.

To my online support network, you were there for me on the days when I doubted myself. Ladies, you are so very important to me. I'm grateful we connected and I can call you my friends.

To the members of my Facebook reader group, *Deb's Bibliomaniacs*, who regularly remind me there are readers out there waiting on my next book. You're the reason I keep writing.

To you, the reader. Thank you for taking a chance on me; for reading my book. I truly appreciate your time. If you've enjoyed reading about Lincoln and Sophie, I'd love to hear from you.

Debra St James is an author of spicy, slow-burn contemporary romance that features cinnamon roll heroes who listen to their women's hearts and their words. She takes her time to weave a detailed tapestry of genuine characters, real-life struggles, love, and romance to create engaging stories that will have you so immersed in the story that you'll never want to leave. Her stories are always guaranteed to take you on an emotional journey that ultimately ends with a HEA!

Debra loves to read romance. Her family often finds her with her nose stuck in her iPad, swooning over her latest book boyfriend. She writes part-time from her Perth home, which she shares with Mr St James and their two sons, whose antics often make her roll her eyes and laugh in equal measure.

Writing a novel had never been on her radar. One morning, she was enjoying a coffee by the river and a story sprouted, seemingly from nowhere. At 51, she pulled up the Pages app on her phone and began to type, giving life to her debut, *Loving Summer*.

The rest, as they say, is history!

www.ingramcontent.com/pod-product-compliance
Lightning Source LLC
Chambersburg PA
CBHW070320190726
48291CB00014B/2389